R. A. MacAvoy's *Tea with the Black Dragon* is the tale of a woman named Martha MacNamara—brought west to San Francisco by her daughter's disappearance—and of the man who changed her life: a mysterious Asian gentleman named Mayland Long who risked his ancient magic powers for her in a battle against modern-day computer wizardry. It is an elegantly crafted contemporary fantasy by a remarkable new writer.

TEA WITH THE BLACK DRAGON
by R. A. MacAvoy

TEA
WITH THE
BLACK DRAGON

R. A. MacAvoy

BANTAM BOOKS
TORONTO • NEW YORK • LONDON • SYDNEY • AUCKLAND

TEA WITH THE BLACK DRAGON
A Bantam Book / May 1983

2nd printing . . . May 1983   4th printing . . . July 1984
3rd printing . . . November 1983   5th printing . . . June 1985

ISBN 0-553-25403-0

Published simultaneously in the United States and Canada

Bantam Books are published by Bantam Books, Inc. Its trademark,
consisting of the words "Bantam Books" and the portrayal of a rooster,
is Registered in U.S. Patent and Trademark Office and in other
countries. Marca Registrada. Bantam Books, Inc., 666 Fifth Avenue,
New York, New York 10103.

PRINTED IN THE UNITED STATES OF AMERICA

O   14 13 12 11 10 9 8 7 6 5

To Ron

Monk: "What is Tao?"

Ts'ao-shan: "A dragon singing in the dry wood."

Monk: "I wonder whether there is anyone who can hear this?"

Ts'ao-shan: "There is no one in the entire world who does not hear this."

Monk: "I do not know what kind of composition the dragon's song is."

Ts'ao-shan: "I also do not know; but all who hear it lose themselves."

The Transmission of the Lamp

1

Martha Macnamara stood at the Pacific, her toes digging into the froth. She had come the length of the country in one day's flight, and she had trouble believing that this was a different ocean.

"Oh go on, admit it," she grumbled, kicking the ivory scum from a pile of kelp. "You're all the same water."

Perhaps not. She peered at the line where the iron blue of the sky hit the soft-colored water. So bare a sky did not shine over Coney Island.

A gull plunged, kissed the water and veered right and away, all ten yards from Mrs. Macnamara. Her head rose to follow its flight and her hands lifted, echoing the bird's gesture. For a moment it seemed her prim figure, gray suited and graying, would fly away into the west—or north along the dirty beach toward the Bridge.

But that was just for a moment, and then the hands touched at the braids that coiled around her head, braids that threatened to slip over her ears.

"If you would know the Way," she recited to herself, "observe the subtlety of water." Martha considered these words as she watched the waves fling themselves roaring onto the sand. What was subtle in such a display of power?

With her round blue eyes very calm in her small round face Mrs. Macnamara watched the ocean. Slowly she smiled.

Where was Liz now—at work? Should Martha try to call again, or wait for her daughter to make the move? After all, Elizabeth had set up the reservation. Martha Macnamara would never have chosen to stay in a place like the James Herald Hotel. Oh, it was comfortable, doubtless, and the only person she had spoken to in the hotel—a bartender—had proven friendly; she had bent his ear for forty minutes at lunch—her dinner, what with the time change—perched on a red leather stool amid black oak and brass, rattling on about airplanes racing the sun, and how the violin had evolved from the viola when Europeans were able to afford carpets and drapes . . . But with the price of a night's lodging at the James Herald she could have bought that bass bow she'd wanted since June.

Martha could just as well have slept on Liz's couch as spent so much of her daughter's money. It was all very strange. The smile disappeared from her lips as she considered how strange. She turned from the water and ascended the sandy slope.

"Mysterious meetings in expensive places," she mumbled as she climbed. A wealth of sand was trapped in her open-toed shoes. "Intrigue. Suspense . . .

"Tune in tonight for shocking revelations!" The sole of her foot gritted against concrete; she stood on the pavement above the beach, emptying her shoes. Except for her gray form, unobtrusive as a rock, the beach was empty on this workday afternoon. Empty and cool. Martha shivered deliciously in the good wool suit she hadn't been able to wear since May.

The Great Highway cut between the City and the Ocean, sharp as the mark of a razor. A young boy ran along the curb, all dressed in white, his feet making a noise like pigeon wings.

Thinking of pigeon wings, Martha's spirits lifted once again. It was her spirits' natural condition, to be lifted. She sprinted across the street in her cordovan brogues, her pleated skirt flapping, receiving the honks of motorists with quiet grace. On the far side—the City side— stood the stand of a pretzel vendor. His teeth flashed at her from a strong, Latin face. She bought a soft pretzel, decorated it with mustard, and ate it where she stood.

Three men walked by together, arm in arm in arm, and then a young woman with bushy hair red as a radish. A bare-chested boy on a spyder bike did wheelies in the street. Honks again. Martha's approval was limitless; San Francisco bid fair to being as zany as New York.

And this was a good corner, probably packed on weekends. Close to downtown yet in sight of the water. She wished she had brought her fiddle. How invigorating to sit down next to the pretzel vendor and play a Bach passacaglia, or maybe a slip jig. Put out the hat. Liz would hate that! Liz behaved with propriety.

Martha Macnamara was smiling again. She licked mustard from her fingers and turned toward the hotel.

She took the stranger's long hand in her own and shook it. "How wonderful! You could span way over two octaves!"

The hand retreated as soon as custom permitted. The owner of it remained standing, a dark figure in the shadow of a paneled wall. He bowed slightly to Mrs. Macnamara.

"Mayland Long . . . Martha Macnamara . . ." The young bartender continued his introduction. "I thought you two should meet."

Both parties stared at him. "Because of the violin," he explained.

"But surely you play keyboards," Martha insisted. "With such a reach . . ."

Mr. Long motioned across the white expanse of table, and did not sit again til Martha had lowered herself into the chair opposite. "Forgive the clutter. I have had a late dinner." He spoke quietly, as empty plates and silver were cleared away before him. "Please have tea with me."

O my, thought the woman to herself. His voice. Lovely English. How wonderful.

"I don't make music," Mr. Long stated. "I merely

appreciate it." He sat in the shadow of his corner table, gazing across to where she sat touched by a beam of light. He saw a slim woman of some fifty years. Her features were small and regular, and her head set well on a slender neck. Her grizzled hair was braided around her head. The hair and her gray wool suit were back lit, causing Martha Macnamara to shine about the edges.

She saw a thin man, dressed darkly, hidden in the dark. The hands stood out against the white linen. They were very dark also, unusually dark, if this man were indeed English. She thought of the beautiful voices of the West Indies. Beautiful, yes, but not correct. Mr. Long's pronunciation was faultless.

"But you, madam," he was saying, "are a creator. I remember you."

"I doubt that!"

"I have a record upstairs in my rooms. A 78. I believe the label is Seraphim. You play, among other things, the Chaconne from the Partita for unaccompanied violin in D minor, by J. S. Bach. I have never heard that piece played better."

He leaned forward as he spoke. Martha Macnamara saw his face.

Her new-built conceptions fell apart as she looked at Mayland Long. The man was Oriental. At least his eyes were. But the rest of him . . . Too long a nose. Too much cheekbone. She gave up trying to place his origin.

"You must be an historian," she laughed. "How many years has it been since they pressed 78s?"

He smiled but did not answer. The tea arrived. Mr. Long poured for her, then for himself. Ignoring the handle on the white china cup he wrapped his hand around it. The thumb overlapped the fingers.

Martha experimented, to see how much of her cup her hands would compass. "Ouch! It's hot!"

"Do not burn yourself, Mrs. Macnamara," said Mr. Long. He smiled with excellent teeth. "I am not an historian—in any organized sense. If you tell me where to find your latest stereo album or Dolby tape, I will bring my collection out of the middle ages."

Martha smiled in turn—not with the smile of flattery well received, but as though she were a child who was about to reveal a naughty secret. It was a smile that made her round face rounder. "Look under the label Ceirníní Claddagh. I play fiddle in a Irish-American Cei li band." Having uttered this, she sat back, wondering if she had become so jaded with the public life—a musician's life—that it was now effortless to talk to strange men alone in strange places. And if she were jaded, then why were Mr. Long's attentions so pleasant?

"Thar Ci'onn! How wonderful," he laughed.

"Oh. You mustn't call my bluff. I speak very little Irish, though I'm taking lessons with a Meath man. He says although my spirit is willing, my accent is very bad. But then music is international, and with a fiddle under my chin I can't talk anyway."

She heard her voice echo through the empty dining room. "And I guess that's the only time I don't. But Mr. Long, I have to ask. Where are you from?"

He glanced into his teacup, then met her blue eyes again. He did not seem offended. "I was born in China," he said. "But I am not entirely—Chinese." Gripping the teapot around its portly middle, he freshened her cup. "What is the name of your ensemble?"

"It's called Linnet's Wings, after a poem by Yeats." She sighed. "Actually, it's a poem Yeats hated . . ."

"I know it," said Mr. Long. " 'There midnight's all a glimmer, and noon a purple glow, and evening full of the linnet's wings.' He had schoolchildren prattling that into his ears for twenty years, so his distaste may be understood."

"I've never been to Innisfree," brooded Martha, staring across the dining room and into the deeper dimness of the bar. She swallowed a yawn. "I don't even know if it's a real place."

The chandeliers were crystal. The tiny drops sparkled in their own light. The weariness of a day's flight blurred her vision, and the play of light reminded her of snow falling into the bright circles of street lights.

But here in San Francisco there was no snow. Never. Just fog and sea. How strange. Unreal.

The voice recalled her. "It is quite real," the voice was saying. She focused again. He meant Innisfree, of course. Not San Francisco.

"You have been to Ireland?" she asked. But she guessed his answer before he could speak.

"What did you do there?"

His eyebrows lifted, and the lean face softened in memories. "I was looking for something." There was a silence Martha allowed to grow. Then he spoke again, with animation.

"Mrs. Macnamara—it is *Mrs*. Macnamara, if I remember?"

"It was."

He did not falter. "Mrs. Macnamara, have you heard the story of Thomas Rhymer?"

"I know the ballad," she admitted. "But it's not Irish."

"That ballad? No. That is Walter Scott. But the story itself is Irish, I believe. It was an Irishman who told it to me.

"Listen!," he began, and as he spoke he stirred his spoon in his cup with a silver sound. Mrs. Macnamara noted this gesture with amusement. She was sure that Mr. Long had not taken sugar.

"You know how Thomas the Rhymer was taken off by the queen of Elfland on her horse of the nine-and-fifty bells. How they swam the river of blood, and how she showed him the roads to heaven and hell, avoiding both of them to take a third. How he served her seven years in delightful capacity, and how in the end his poor reward was that he was made incapable of lying. This much is what got back to Scott."

"There is more?"

"Obviously. The ballad is cut off just where it becomes interesting. It does not touch on the predicament of a bard bereft of his stock in trade—flattery. It does not so much as mention the Rhymer's son."

Mr. Long straightened in his chair, thereby disappearing into shadow. His hands touched together and then opened, as though he were releasing a bird into the air. "Thomas Rhymer," he stated, "had a son by the queen of Elfland. The boy was five years old when his father's term ended and the Rhymer was sent upon his way." Mr. Long paused, breathed deeply and stared into the air above Martha's head.

"Thomas left, but he came back again, fording the river of blood, blundering through the tangle of green which hides that road from mortal eyes. It was not so pleasant a journey for a man alone, but Thomas Rhymer found his way back to the land of the not-so-blessed and he stole his little son away."

"No. I've never heard this," whispered Martha Macnamara. "Have you got the verses?"

He stopped and drew breath. "There are verses," he admitted. "But I don't sing. Humor me."

And he continued. "Back in the world again, Thomas Rhymer took to his trade, and the lad went with him. But fortune no longer smiled upon him."

"Because he couldn't lie."

"Quite likely, Mrs. Macnamara. And before the year was out, the Rhymer began to hear the wailing of the Sidhe in the night and he knew he was hunted."

"Oh no!" exclaimed Mrs. Macnamara, finding herself moved, almost frightened. It was that voice . . .

"Hiding the boy at the monastery at Lagan—this was in the days Cormac O'Dubh was Abbot—he rode off, leading the hunt away.

"Crofters heard the racket of his horse's hoofs pass in the early night, but in the coldest hour they saw the passage of riders who made no sound, a company with faces like chalk and horses shining without moonlight. This part of it has been remembered in Lagan Valley from then til now.

"In the last hour before dawn this ghastly company arrayed itself before the gates of the monastery, and she who led them threw down upon the grass the body of Thomas. Knowing she could not storm such a stronghold of the new faith she offered a trade: her son for the small breath of life she had left in the father.

"Cormac himself stood at the gate. He was a burly Abbot. He cried out that he would pray for souls, but he could not sell them.

"But out from the gate squirmed the boy himself, and he ran to his father and knelt beside him. Spurring her horse the queen plucked up her son. In the same moment Abbot Cormac O'Dubh ran out from the monastery gate to Thomas Rhymer. Him he took and carried to safety behind the gates.

"But even this is not the end of the story. For the queen of Elfland, chalk faced on her pale horse, let out a wail of anger, and she held the boy at arm's length from her, and she put him down from her horse.

" 'He stinks!' she cried. 'He stinks of the dove! My boy, ma'cushla! Heart of my heart, has been dipped in the filthy bowl!'

"And all the shining horses reared up and sank into the earth, and the Sidhe were gone.

"Because the good Abbot had put the boy beyond the reach of his mother's people as long as time holds sway. He had baptized him."

"Ah! Of course." Martha hit her palm against the table. "The obvious solution. I never thought of it.

"But Thomas Rhymer . . . he's alive? I mean, he *was* alive after that?"

"He lived. He was a very quiet man in later years."

Mayland Long stared into the depths of an empty cup.

"I believe you have that tale from Thomas Rhymer himself," said Martha. "You tell it with such . . .

authority." She sighed, once more aware of the time change. While Mr. Long was speaking she had forgotten she was tired.

"From the Rhymer?" He leaned forward and lifted his eyebrows in mock wonderment. "How could that be?"

"He was unconscious during the crux of the story. I have the story from the boy, of course. The Rhymer's son.

"Beautiful boy," he added, after a moment. "Resembled his mother."

Martha blinked twice. The hour and the moment combined to overwhelm her. Cradling her head in her arms she laughed until she hiccupped.

"Forgive me—I'm tired. Jet lag. I'd better turn in now. Getting up at five." This last word dissolved into a yawn.

As she pulled herself to her feet Mr. Long rose also. "You will remain through tomorrow, though?" He spoke with some alarm. "I have not let you talk about your music. You must join me for dinner."

She put her hand to the gray braid above her ear and scratched thoughtfully. "Tomorrow I'm supposed to meet my daughter. That's why I flew in. But she hasn't called yet, and I can't reach her. Can I call you sometime in the middle of the day?"

"Certainly. My schedule is not crowded; if I am not in my rooms, you can leave a message at the desk."

His voice pulled at her once again as she turned to leave the table. "Mrs. Macnamara. Why so early? Why five o'clock?"

"I sit," she called back. "Zazen."

Mayland Long stood alone beside the empty cups. "Zazen?" he whispered to himself. His dark face was lit with an amusement which grew and deepened.

The bartender stopped her on the stair. "Mr. Trough," she greeted him, and continued walking.

"Jerry," he corrected. "Can you spare two minutes?"

"Just about," Martha smiled, and putting the key to her door, she ushered the young man in.

Martha's rooms were not the largest nor the most opulent in the James Herald Hotel. Had Martha herself made the reservations, they would have been the cheapest. As it was, she had a bed-sitting room with three chairs, all of which were too large and too soft to be comfortable and a canopy bed that dwarfed her.

Jerry Trough was still clutching a damp bar towel in one hand. He sought for a place to put it down, rejecting the walnut table, the quilted satin spread, the brocade seat of a side chair. At last he dropped it to the carpet, where it lay by an open suitcase which spilled over with white cotton underwear and paperback books. He cleared his throat.

"I saw you leave the dining room and wanted to catch you before you turned in. It's about the man I introduced to you tonight."

She turned quickly, leaning her hip against the Chippendale reproduction dresser. "Mr. Long? Yes, we talked an hour away. What about him?"

"What did you think of him?"

She smiled at the impudence of the question. "I found him informative and entertaining. Not to mention exotic. I may have supper with him tomorrow."

"Watch out," mumbled the bartender. "I know. He can be a real—actor, and all. Loads of fun. He's a friend of mine, too, in a way." Trough shifted from foot to foot.

"Just 'in a way?' " Her eyebrows lifted interrogatively.

Trough shrugged. "Okay. He is a friend. But I ask you to be careful, Martha. I don't think he's quite all there."

"Mr. Long?" Her voice rose in consternation. "I've rarely met anyone more—more *there*. More present, I mean." She glared at the bartender. "If the man is schizophrenic or something like that, why did you introduce me to him?"

As though Martha's outrage had shaken the starch out of him, Jerry Trough sat down on the edge of the bed. His eyes darted about the room and he laced his hands together. "I told you why. Because of the violin. And because you're a lot alike in other ways."

"Oh. I'm a nut too?" Martha's eyes went even wider, and she put her hands on her hips.

The young man sighed and ran his fingers through his curly black hair. "Of course not. You take me wrong. What I mean is that you both seem to like . . . conversation. Have large vocabularies. And you're both alone —you because you just got here, and he because . . . he just is.

"And when I see you get excited about little things. Like the way you talked about racing the sun in the airplane and almost winning except you had to stop at the end of the country. Well, Mr. Long's like that too; he's got these old, falling apart books of Chinese poetry he says nobody's ever translated before, and he brings them to the bar and sets them down and scribbles in little notebooks. He gets excited about it, but I never hear about his translations getting printed anywhere, so I don't know . . .

"I used to think he was really stuffy until I noticed that half of everything he said was a pun or a joke. You're somewhere around the same age . . . I think . . ." Here Trough's words faded. He knew himself to be treading shaky ground on the subject of age.

"So I thought he'd interest you—to talk to for a few minutes. But Mr. Long . . . I want you to know if you get him drunk," Trough said, "Old Mr. Long will tell you that he used to be a dragon. And he's not joking around when he says it."

Martha pushed off from the dresser and came to stand beside the awkward young man. On her face a triumphant smile was blossoming.

Trough regarded his own feet as he continued. "He told me he used to be ten yards long and solid black, with a head like a chrysanthemum. Not any other flower—he insisted it was a chrysanthemum. He also thought it was important I knew that he had had five toes on each foot. As a dragon, that is."

The worry had cleared from Martha's brow. "Oh!" she breathed. "I see. Well, Jerry, me boy. This night he told *me* that he was personally acquainted with Thomas Rhymer.

"Or at least knew his son," truth compelled her to add.

Trough stared blankly. "And he doesn't?"

"Not likely. But don't you see where his head is at, when he says things like that?"

"No. Where?"

She gestured in the air above her head, as though calling all available Muses to her aid. "Why he's . . . exercising a scholarly imagination. He's smashing the world, to recreate it in his own pattern. That man is an artist, and conversation is his medium.

"If he appears a bit crazy it's only because he's too much alone," she concluded. "I understand him. Or I think I do. I can't explain any better than that." Her blue eyes stared at the carpet, the pile of books, the wet bar towel . . .

The bartender stood up. "Still, be careful, Martha. They found a body in the hall last year, in front of his door."

Martha Macnamara took Trough's place on the bed. It bounced. "What? A body? Whose?"

"The dead guy was a junkie, I heard. Police record long as your arm. No loss to San Francisco, I guess, but that was just a freaky way to find him, you know? No marks, no blood, just his neck bone snapped. Coroner decided he fell, but why he was there in the first place, and why he should fall so hard he broke his neck . . ."

Here the bartender stopped portentously.

"So you think poor Mr. Long is a secret killer, do you? He's part Chinese—perhaps he knows some deadly Oriental way to kill a man from behind a wooden door. Perhaps he's the head of a Tong!" Eyes flashing, Martha rose to her feet.

"I rather like *old* Mr. Long," she stated. "He may tell me that he used to be a dragon, or will be a dragon come Tuesday next, or that he actually *is* a dragon underneath his suit jacket and white shirt-front. I will try to receive such a confidence in the spirit in which it is given."

She paused for breath, and her bright outrage flowed away from her. She regarded the bartender more calmly. "And I doubt very much that you'll find me in the hallway outside his door, dead with no marks of violence."

Mr. Trough shrugged an ineloquent shrug. "Sure. You're safe, I guess. Besides, he never drinks much with dinner." Martha's irritated frown sent Trough out the door.

She put her face between the panels of the drape and rested her forehead against cool glass. Outside the city swept twinkling north and west to the sea. No snow. Also no fog.

That little interview had almost ruined her mood. She decided she wouldn't let it. After all, she was in San Francisco neither to fight nor frolic, but to talk to Liz, who evidently had problems and wanted her advice. Martha had been able to give her daughter little enough as a child—surely she could now spare a week and a little maternal concern. Regardless of impudent bartenders. Regardless of fascinating men.

Where was Liz's apartment? San Mateo. That was south. Behind the hotel. She could not play the game of pretending to locate her daughter among the lights below.

Was Liz nervous also? Sleepless? Afraid of the interview for which she'd called her mother clear across the continent? That would be unlike Liz. She was probably sleeping soundly, believing her mother was getting in on a late flight. Or she could be out on a date, or what was most likely of all, at work amid a clatter of computers. Liz would get in touch.

She turned from the window and yawned. Her thoughts returned to the man she had met tonight. What a wonderful voice. Impossible hands. And that strange hybrid face, falling in and out of shadow.

It was easier to think of this brief acquaintance than it was to think of her daughter. Easier and more fun.

She caught a glimpse of herself in the dresser mirror. One of her braids was falling over her ear. She shook her head dubiously at her image. She could not see herself a remarkable beauty.

Yet Mr. Long—she felt—liked her. He knew who she was. He was interested to know more. Her gaze searched the mirror.

So he has an old 78 and a good memory—the mirror told her. And he likes an audience. Her shoulders sagged as she kicked off her shoes.

But in five seconds this depression also vanished, swept away in the tides of Martha's good humor. She threw off the tweed suit and stepped out of her underwear. Stark naked, she dialed the switchboard and asked for a wake-up call at five.

In darkness, leaning against a wall of red brocade, Mayland Long waited for the elevator. He smiled, and his teeth glinted in the greenish light of the control buttons.

Zen. . . . to have come so far, to this stone city where the ocean was on the wrong side of the sun, to wait and watch himself age with cruel speed, foreign in form, in speech, in feeling. . . . Here to find again the trace of his own interminable, floundering search. And in such unlikely shape as that of Martha Macnamara.

Ch'an.

There was that odor about her: not a sweetness, exactly, but a wildness suggesting breezes that have touched cold water and living wood. The air surrounding Martha Macnamara was charged with . . . reality. Unpronounceable reality: Long could feel her reality against his face like sunlight or rain. Her every gesture had spoken to him in certainty, yet she had expressed no opinions, leaving such pronouncements to him.

Martha had something which drew him to her, like a wondering beast to the fires of men. She had what he lacked, in her laughter, her simplicity, her quick passions, her certainty. It was the taste of existence—of being.

It was the Tao.

His breath escaped slowly between his teeth. He wanted to see her again, and feared chance would not allow it. Out of habit he tamped down that desire, attempting to snuff it before it could do him harm. He would see her or he would not; pain was irrelevant to the future.

The elevator shuddered open. It was bright inside, and empty. He stepped in and pressed the button for the seventh floor. Memories competed with the drum of the motor.

Old hands. The smell of rain—the smell of Ch'an. Quiet words in rough Cantonese. "I am not to be your master. Your master has to be stronger than you are—has to tell you you are a fool and make you to know it. And make you feel content in being a fool. How could I do that for you? I'm old. You are too strong for me; you are full of *chi*." The old man had paused then, huddled against the wind while clouds thickened above them.

"I will tell you this, Long," he continued. "Before you find yourself you will lose your *chi*. Also you will leave behind you all pride of body, pride of mind. You will be reduced. Like me." The old man closed his eyes, and rain began to beat against his gray, crew-cut hair. He pulled his coat closer. Suddenly his eyes snapped open and he looked Long in the face.

"You must leave China. Go across the ocean. There you will meet your master." He set down his teacup with a palsied hand. His voice rose, grew fierce.

"I tell you this, most honored and impressive visitor. You are a fool, yes, but you will find the very thing you seek. You will find truth!"

Mayland Long stepped out of the elevator. The words of the old man faded. They had been polished by repetition in his mind til they gleamed gray: links of iron, beads on a chain. They were a string of beads that

Long told daily, while he waited and studied and thought.

He yawned and felt for his key. He didn't want to think any more. He'd rather tell stories to Martha.

2

The James Herald Hotel stood on a high slope of Nob Hill. The sea wind broke upon it like the Pacific broke over the shore rocks that were visible from the hotel's upper windows. It was built of brick, but its ground floor was encased with brass and varnished teak. All its myriad windows were shining. The James Herald was not the oldest of the great San Francisco hotels and it was not the largest. It was, however, old enough and large enough. In Martha Macnamara's opinion, it was quite expensive enough, also.

The cut glass doors to the dining room stood open. An August evening light, admitted through the tall leaded windows beyond, filtered into the hallway where she stood. The angles in the glass doors cut the light sharply. The crystal chandeliers, too, sparkled painfully sharp and exact this evening. Tiny pendants emitted a spectrum of color. They would provide her no soft visions of snow tonight.

She sought around the room, among the glistening white circles of linen, looking for a man alone. There were few of those; the Crystal Room was not a place where one ate alone.

Yet he did. Mr. Long lived at the James Herald Hotel and took his meals in the dining room. Both these things were very strange. Martha could bring to mind places in San Francisco where she would rather eat—Henry

Africa, where the window was gilt with the motto *Vive la mort, vive la guerre, vive la légion étrangère,* and young men, brittle and elegant, stood warily around the door, or the fast-food stall in Japantown, where the cookies were pressed in the shape of a fish. And Martha had only arrived in the city yesterday. Eating in the Crystal Room's icy splendor every evening didn't say much for Mr. Long. Where was he, anyway? Had she been stood up twice in one day?

As she passed between the glass doors, a dark shape welled out of the shadows. "Ah!" she began, but it was not Mayland Long, but the Maitre d'. "I'm just looking for someone," she explained, as the man bowed stiffly from the waist, like a bird. She restrained an impulse to return the bow.

"Mrs. Macnamara?" he addressed her. "Please come with me."

She followed, her eyebrows drawn down and together. Martha Macnamara did not like being known to people whom she did not know. It made her feel unpleasantly like a child. She contemplated asking the Maitred' his name, but if she did that she was certain he would give her his first name alone, and she would then have to insist he call her Martha. And she did not really want to be called Martha by this man, who would then continue to call all other customers by their surnames. She remained silent.

Mayland Long sat at a table beneath a window full of sky. It was a very good table, and its desirability impressed upon Martha that Mr. Long was a wealthy man.

He rose from his seat as he saw her approach, and he too bowed to her. Mrs. Macnamara lost all restraint. Placing her palms together she bowed in turn. The Maitre'd held her chair.

She greeted him with a smile. "Wonderful weather, today," she began. "Clear and crisp."

Affably, he nodded. "Of course. The rainy season hasn't started yet."

"Did I scandalize the poor man with my gassho?" she asked, as soon as they were alone.

He responded slowly, as though she had broached a subject of some depth. "Scandalize? How can one scandalize a maitre d'hotel? Such a man has seen it all before. And if one did succeed in subjecting him to scandal, I don't believe his face would express his condition. Did you intend to scandalize Jean-Pierre?"

The voice was the same. Her memory had not added quality. "No. But I can take only so much bowing before I bow back. Is he really Jean-Pierre?"

He considered the question. "To the best of my knowledge he is. Jean-Pierre Burrell. Father of five. Canadian by birth. I believe he has managed the floor in the Crystal Room for over ten years."

Mr. Long leaned back in his chair and regarded his dinner companion. Sunlight fell slanting across his face.

His eyes, she thought. Last night she had seen them as solid black-brown. Chinese eyes. Today they were not opaque. Light entered the iris and was trapped in it, glowing. Almost amber, like the sun through a beer bottle.

And he was letting her see him—hands, face and all. He did not court mystery. Martha was very glad of this; she had no patience with mystery.

"I am very sorry your daughter failed to show," Mr. Long continued, as he looked in turn at Martha. She was wearing a plain blue dress and her eyes were blue. Sunlight or moonlight, Martha Macnamara's eyes were always blue. "Is this something one can expect, with her?"

A frown imprinted itself on her round, innocent features. "No. Not at all. Liz is very—reliable. Almost too much so. She wants things done right. She keeps all her shoes in the pockets of a big plastic bag hanging in her closet. And she believes in independence for women."

She stared at the menu with sightless eyes. "That's why we don't get along, I guess."

Mr. Long smiled slowly. "You don't approve of your daughter's views, Mrs. Macnamara? I would have thought a lady of such independent spirit . . ."

She waved his words aside. "Oh, no. I approve of Liz. I wouldn't dare do otherwise. It's she who disapproves of me."

His eyebrows drew together. "Then I am at a loss. Please explain."

She drew a deep breath as her fingers played with her water glass. It was cut crystal, of course.

"Liz disapproved of my cutting off my—my musical career to raise a child."

Delight etched Mr. Long's lean face. "A child? Do you mean Elizabeth herself?"

"Exactly. She feels she is a sort of involuntary accomplice in my oppression. And, she feels I caved in, when I should have fought."

"How should you have fought?" He leaned forward, hands wrapped together on the table.

He can't be more than sixty, considered Mrs. Macnamara. Probably younger, though it's so hard to tell with Eurasians. Too young to retire. Too young to live in a hotel and eat in the Crystal Room every night.

"I should have continued in the job I was educated for, playing Bach and Berlioz in long dresses. I should have left her with a nanny, or even had an abortion, though that was a very different story in those days.

"At any rate, she is sure I shouldn't be wasting my time playing fiddle in an Irish band, touring about and sleeping in the living rooms of friends. Not at my age."

"And what age is that?" he asked blandly. A challenge hid somewhere within the question, and his brown eyes hid within their creases.

Easily she answered, "I'm fifty. How old are you?"

Mayland Long threw back his head and laughed. His teeth were large and very white against his skin. "Older than you are, Mrs. Macnamara. And more vain. I won't answer that question just now."

Then he leaned forward again. His elongated fingers

stretched across the menu he had not opened. He touched her pink hand for just a moment. "But I think it would be wonderful to fiddle with the Linnet's Wings and sleep wherever one finds oneself. At any age."

She found herself saying, "Then why not do it, Mr. Long. I know you're not a musician. I don't mean that. I mean . . . Why do you live here, in this beautiful, boring hotel? And why do you eat . . . here? In the Crystal Room. Every night. When you are . . ." she finished with quiet intensity ". . . who you are."

He drew back, his two hands flat on the tablecloth. I have offended him, thought Martha. She watched.

"And who is that?" he asked softly, but he gave her no time to answer. "There is time," he continued, in the same tone of voice: softly, very softly. "There is time for the James Herald, too, in a long life. Sometimes one must wait for things."

Wait for what? she thought, but did not continue her attack. "Forgive me if I was out of line. I spoke on impulse."

The light was failing outside. The chandeliers cast haloes against the beamed ceiling. Mr. Long nodded. "Impulse or instinct. I am not offended, Mrs. Macnamara."

She did not quite understand. She opened her menu and stared, seeing nothing.

"There is something marvelous in formality," she murmured. "Greetings. Bows. And surnames." She gave up searching among the cuts of beef and lamb. She looked at him again. "But I'm a poor peasant, really. I can't be Mrs. Macnamara for more than a half hour at a time before I get giddy."

She found herself saying the words she had swallowed earlier in front of the Maitre d'. "Please call me Martha." Then she quailed before his silence, realizing she could no more call this man by his first name than she could fly.

"I don't ask the privilege in return," she qualified. "Especially since you admit to being older than me."

It was his turn to concern himself with a water glass.

He held it up to the last light of day. "Why? Am I so stuffy, Martha?"

"No. Not stuffy," Her forehead creased. She searched for the word. "Intimidating."

"But not too intimidating to have my ear twisted for living in a comfortable hotel. For dining at the same place nightly." He lowered the crystal to the table. The corners of his mouth turned upwards.

"There are very few people who call me by my given name. I don't know why that should be, but it's true."

"Isn't that the way you want it?"

He shook his head. The smile widened. "I . . . don't have an opinion on the matter. And you . . ." He adopted the imperturbability of a stage Chinaman, "Must decide for me what I am to be called from this moment foward. And where I—"

The waiter interrupted, letting Mrs. Macnamara blush in comparative privacy. She chose the lobster. Given the choice, she almost always picked the lobster. Mr. Long asked for rock cod. Rock cod was not on the menu, but the waiter merely nodded and inquired about the wine.

It was dark out now. The window was shiny black, and whatever crisis had been approaching had passed away with the waiter. Mr. long was eager to talk about Buddhism. Martha tried to listen, but her mind drifted back to Liz. She vacillated between being annoyed with her daughter for this cavalier treatment and being very anxious for her. Being annoyed was by far the most comfortable feeling.

"I used to have quite a collection of the commentaries of Nagarjuna," he began. "Are you interested in the Indians?"

She shook her head and hurried to swallow a bite of romaine. "I have no head for philosophy. I get confused."

He lay down his knife and fork neatly. Martha withstood five seconds of silent scrutiny. "I see," he said finally. "Zen."

"Whatever word you like. I sit still, or I try. Truth is

what is important, and writings just . . . catch me by the heels. I think Bodhidharma has the right attitude, to sit for nine years facing a wall. Truth!" she sighed, gesturing helplessly. Her fork clinked and rolled into her salad bowl.

"He fascinated me," admitted Mr. Long. He stared over his shoulder into the black glass. "I used to watch him from where he couldn't see me. Or so I thought."

"What was this?" Martha groped, her mind skipping tracks as she listened.

"Bodhidharma. Sitting by the rock wall of a cave, in Honan. Sometimes he sat in full lotus, but more often he tucked under his right foot. Sometimes he wrapped a blanket around him, and the snow would make a mound over his head.

"But it would burn off. The snow—or rain, as the season dictated—would melt and turn to steam and the blanket would smell of scalded wool. That is probably what called the man to my attention first. Burning off the snow." Mayland Long opened his eyes very wide as his gaze slid from the window to the intent face of Martha Macnamara. "I was not always—subtle—you know. That comes with age, if we are fortunate. But two things I have ever respected are warmth and the ability to sit still."

Martha listened to him speak. She had a peculiar skill at listening which was in no way to be confused with an aversion to talking herself. Her listening had an intensity which reached out into the speaker and eased the meaning from him, which knitted word to word beyond the first mere intent which called him to speak. She listened—as she moved—with grace.

And she noticed, in passing, that Mr. Long had scarcely touched his wine.

"I don't know where the story began that the man called Bodhidharma was a frog-faced ogre. He was a small man—an Indian, of course. But he was quite courteous.

"Courteous to me, at least," he added. Then there was

silence between them till the gentle pull of Martha's listening was felt again.

"I waited for him to speak." He chuckled and touched the bright blade of the butter knife. "I did not cut off my arm to impress him. I don't know who it was who did that, if indeed that story is not pure fabrication. I merely waited to be noticed. All the winter and most of spring.

"I waited . . ." Mayland Long's head rose up and his eyes met that peaceful, blue, inescapable listening. "I have been waiting so very long, Martha," he said.

She only nodded.

Once again they were saved—or lost—by the arrival of the waiter bearing the entree. The placing of the dishes entailed a certain amount of bustle.

Plates were lifted and lowered. Silver winked in the light and the knives made a sweet tinkle against one another. Behind all this Mayland Long sat patiently still, having uttered a confession, and having that confession erased by events. His face was touched with loss.

On the other side of the mild turmoil sat Martha. Her smile grew as the waiter receded. It was a smile which committed Mayland Long to nothing, welcoming all.

He glanced down at his plate. The fish filet was wound around itself, skewered and dusted with paprika. The potatoes came out of a pastry gun. "When must you leave?" he asked.

Martha stared with true interest at her lobster. It was enormous and red. She realized the depths of her folly then, and wished for a bib.

"I will leave when I find her," she spoke with a grim determination which owed something to her feelings concerning the dead crustacean before her.

"Then I may arrange to have her kidnapped." Mr. Long spoke quietly, almost to himself. Martha, attacking a bulbous scarlet claw, seemed not to hear.

"Where does she live?"

"Umph! This is impossible," Martha muttered, as a steak knife slipped in her now-greasy hand. "I'm not fit for this sort of establishment. Don't they believe in using nutcrackers, Mayland?"

"Allow me." He pulled her plate to the center of the table, where with his fingertips he curled the shell back from the meat as though it were paper. "There is no delicate way to eat a lobster." In this manner, the new intimacy of his given name passed without comment.

"Where does she live, your daughter?"

Martha sighed, picking at her food. "I don't know," she admitted. "She used to work for FSS, in San Mateo, or so she told me. I called them. The switchboard said there was no one by the name Macnamara."

Mayland Long's eyebrows lifted, and his eyes glittered with a harder sort of light. "Ah!" he said. "We have a puzzle.

"Tell me, Martha, what does Elizabeth do for a living?"

Martha swallowed a bite of lobster. It was very good, but it was a Maine lobster and not native to this seacoast at all. It arrived by plane, as did Martha. Perhaps the same plane.

"She's a systems analyst. FSS stands for Financial Systems Software. She went to Stanford in math." She was reminded that her dinner companion was Chinese by the fact that his face, open so recently, had gone completely unreadable to Martha. She watched and waited.

"A systems analyst? Umm. Systems analysts rarely call their parents from across the country with mysterious problems. Still more rarely do they disappear. It is not part of the technical mentality to disappear.

"How will you go about finding her?"

Martha Macnamara's unobtrusive chin attempted to assert itself. "I will start by renting a car and buying an area map. I will drive down to Financial Systems Software. If they cannot or will not help me I proceed to Stanford University and seek out Auld Acquaintance. Hers, not mine. If I fail there, I try an old address I have. She moved about six months ago and was staying with a friend from college while she tried to buy a condo; I have that girl's number, but no one ever answers there."

She shook her head admiringly. "Just think of it! She's not twenty-five yet, and buying a condo. Without help, of course—I don't have a nickel."

"If that doesn't work, and she hasn't called in a few days, then I go to the police."

He paused before speaking. "Is it so serious?"

"She told me she was in trouble. She said I was not to know where she lived because she was . . . nervous . . . about somebody. What am I to think? A pesky boyfriend? Bills?

"I don't know *what* to think," she concluded.

Mayland Long folded his hands together. "No use to draw conclusions amid such a lack of data." He regarded nothing, intently.

"Martha—what do you know about your daughter's line of work. About computers?"

"Me? Why, nothing. They send bills. They eat my little bank card and give me money—when they're working."

"Then, may I be permitted to assist you?"

She started in surprise. "Help me find Elizabeth? That would be too much to . . ." Her face lit in wonder. "Do you mean that you know about computers, too, as well as Ireland and China?"

He shrugged. His shoulders were thin beneath his excellently fitted suit jacket. "A language is a language."

Mayland Long entered his suite of rooms and closed the door behind him. The sitting room was neat and sparsely furnished, with a pair of wing-back Queen Anne chairs set beside the bay window, a sofa of similar design before the swept and evidently useable fireplace, and a single table of black lacquerwork standing between the two chairs. On this table lay an oilcloth pad, and upon that rested a hot plate, a red kettle and a jade-green teapot. The striking feature of this room was its walls, which were covered floor to ceiling with books. Wherever space and the angles of the room permitted stood high, heavy book cupboards, some with glass doors. Elsewhere single shelves were drilled into the plaster, and atop all, near the high ceiling, piles of books ascended, stacked flat.

The books in Mr. Long's room were a motley crew, being old or new, soiled or stiff and clean, composed in equal numbers of leather binding and bright paperback.

There was one other object of note in this idiosyncratic chamber, and that was a bronze statue, one meter high, which sat on a shelf at eye-level: a lacuna in the wall of books. It was the figure of a Chinese dragon. The creature sat up on its hind legs, in a manner reminiscent of the caterpillar in *Alice*. It held in its left hand a tiny and exquisite teacup, and in its right a saucer. Its tail curled around in front, like a third hand, and held open a book. The entire statue was brassy black except for the eyes, which were polished and lacquered and shone like gold.

Mayland Long paced to the low shelves beneath the window. Searching through the row of books, his hand reached out and began to harvest. First he found the three volumes of Knuth's *The Art of Computer Programming*, *Principles of Compiler Design*, and the *Conference Proceedings of the Third West Coast Computer Faire*. Then, rising with this armload, he made his way to a large, slotted magazine rack, whence he plucked out *Dr. Dobb's Journal of Computer Calisthenics and Orthodontia*.

He lowered this accretion of technical expertise to the seat of one of the chairs and, picking it up by the carved wooden arms, so as not to damage the Turkish rug, he placed it next to the other chair, on which he sat.

A tall lamp stood beside him; he snapped it on. He grunted briefly as he opened Knuth, vol. I, *Fundamental Algorithms*: a happy little sound, full of contentment.

3

With reddening fingers Martha pried apart the loops of her key ring and forced the keys of the rental car upon it. She had reached the landing between the third and fourth floors and stopped to breathe for a moment before continuing her ascent. She wondered what sprite had tempted her to hoof it from the lobby to the seventh floor, where Mayland Long resided. Surely it was not the spirit of physical fitness. Health trailed along in Martha Macnamara's wake; she had never turned to pursue it.

She snorted as she recognized her motive. She was visiting a man's rooms alone, and so had unconsiously avoided observation. What an absurd right hemisphere you have, she railed at herself. Nasty half-brain. Sneaky and absurd . . . Serve it right to climb the rest of the way.

She stood at the top. "There," she mumbled to herself. "See what you made me do?"

The plain iron sign read seventh floor. She leaned against a newell post cast in the shape of an acorn, feeling the heat in her face. She stepped through the fire door into the hall.

Here, somewhere along the maroon turkish-patterned runner, was where the body was found. The junkie. With his neck broken. She ought to ask him about that story— get it over with and out of her mind.

Lifting her hand to knock on the door marked 714 cost a great effort of will. She stared at the shiny brass numbers. Heavy. Solid. 7-1-4. Her face was still hot; he would think she were blushing. Perhaps she was. Definitely she would *not* ask about the body.

She listened for movement within and heard nothing. Then the door softly opened, revealing Mr. Long. He balanced a cup on a saucer in his left hand. In the morning light he looked thinner and less exotic. Standing in shirtsleeves between Martha and the window, he seemed very slight indeed.

"Looking for bloodstains?" he asked gently, smiling. He laughed at her reaction. "Forgive me, Martha. That unfortunate accident is our one piece of notoriety at the James Herald. Everyone who speaks to Jerry Trough finds out about it."

"Did you see the body, Mayland? It must have lain just outside your door."

He shook his head. "No. I slept through the entire incident. I had been out late the night before, you see, and only woke when the police started knocking on doors. Couldn't help them."

She stood in the doorway, blinking all around at the book-lined room. Mayland Long lifted his suit jacket from the closer of the two wing-back chairs and gestured her to sit.

She noted the teacup, and the fact that his shirt cuffs were not buttoned. "Sorry. I guess I'm on time." She snorted in self-deprecation as she lowered herself into the delicate chair. "Unforgivable, really. You become so used to people being twenty minutes late that you tack that time onto the real time you want them to be there and then someone like me comes along and ruins everyone's schedule. It's because I'm so literal minded."

"Never apologize," said Long. "Especially not for punctuality. I was not underway as early as you this morning, but that ought to give you cause for resentment, not me." He placed the saucer and cup neatly on the floor, atop the second volume of Knuth. "I have only just gotten out of the shower.

"Please pour yourself a cup of tea while I finish straightening up. It is not black but Chinese," he added, and knelt beneath the window, paging books carefully into their shelves.

It was the tea, she discovered, which was not black but Chinese. Smelled like peaches. Tasted slightly salty. As she sat, craning her neck to stare all around, she began to swing her legs. The chair was too high for her. It made her feel like a little girl.

So did all this room, so old looking—old mannish looking, really, but in such good taste. And almost oppressively neat by her standards. Having a few books scattered across the floor proved the rest weren't just book-binding wallpaper.

Martha Macnamara was resigned to being too early. She sat swinging her stockinged legs while her toes brushed the subtle cream and maroon pattern of the rug.

Mayland Long did not mention that he himself hadn't shut eye the past night, and if weariness caught him as he squatted on the floor, slipping *Dr. Dobb's* between *Donleavy's* and *Forbes* September 4th issues, that drowse might have been merely the effect of the first sunlight, which struck suddenly through the morning haze and threw him into a sort of peaceful trance. His amber eyes lidded over and his hand was slipping down the slots of the rack when he heard Martha gasp. Then his head moved quickly.

"That is Oolong," he stated.

The half empty cup and saucer rattled in her lap. "No," she whispered eagerly. "The statue! That magnificent statue!"

He turned back to the window, brushing invisible dust from his trouser knees. "Yes. It's called Oolong." His perfect voice had sunk to a mumble of disinterest and Mayland Long stared out into the sky, caught by some pattern of sun and mist.

"Is that the name of the piece, the sculptor, or the dragon who posed for it?"

Motionless, he answered, "Any one you please," and

he yawned an enormous yawn, with his tongue curling up like that of a cat. But when he turned again toward her there was crispness and decision in his attitude.

"Now, my dear lady, I have done with dawdling and we may off."

"Ah. Okay." She deposited her white cup on the oilcloth beside the green teapot and the red kettle. Puzzled, she lifted the lid of the pot and the smell of leaves leaked out. She was sure that tea was Oolong. Both the tea *and* the statue were named Oolong? The tea, the statue *and* the dragon? The word swelled in her mind, assuming awful proportions. Perhaps if she asked him the name of the black lacquer table here, he would state, "Oolong" again. She had once had a Master like that; no matter what the question was, his answer had been, "Dust on the floor." After a year of that she had rebelled, shouting, "There's nothing *in* you but 'Dust on the floor!'" That had turned out to be the proper response; from then on they'd gotten along famously.

She met Long's challenging eyes with a greater challenge. "Oolong," she announced. "The tea, the statue, the dragon—and you too. The same word can do for all." And she laughed, till the bare shock in his face drained the humor away.

"I'm not insane, really," she explained carefully. "That was just a little Zennie joke. Very little.

"And now, Holmes! The hunt's afoot! Or the game's up, or . . . something . . ." She preceded a thoughtful Mayland Long out the door.

"When Thou hast done, Thou art not done, for I have more," he announced, sinking back into the upholstery of the passenger seat. Brown fingers, seemingly by themselves, sought out the handle of the door and swung it closed.

Martha was a bit dejected, having drawn a blank both at FSS and Stanford. What was worse, Judy Freeman,

Liz's school friend and Martha's best hope, had moved to Seattle months previously.

She started the engine of the silver Mercury Zephyr and lurched into first gear. Her passenger was uneffected by the jerk; he had had his arm braced against the dash. It was not the first lurch of the day.

"Done? Oh yes. Donne. That's John Donne, isn't it? Punning as usual. When I was first at school, everyone was mad about Donne. Now dropped like a stone. Sign of the times, I guess."

Mayland Long cast a cold eye in her direction. "You insist on dating me, madam."

With complete frankness she said, "Yes. I would love to. Hate mysteries, and you insist on being one. But I like Donne. '. . . outside that room, Where I shall be Thy music, I pause to tune my instrument before . . .' or something.

"But tell me, Mayland. What is the More? I find the only child of my flesh has no job, no friends, no forwarding address. She had grown into a positive nonentity, if that is not too much of a paradox. How do we find her?"

Long glanced at her face and read her concern. He didn't reply immediately. The date palms of Palm Drive passed by the windows of the car: tall ones and short ones, the sick and the healthy, dead nubs and towering majesties. He peered through them at the road ahead. "Please turn right on El Camino," he said.

"Yessir." She did so.

"You'll find her, Martha," said Long quietly. "You always find the thing you look for in the last place you look."

Laughter caught her unaware. She shifted lanes. "My! Look at these bicyclists! How pretty they are. All blond. And such muscles. Stanford has always had good-looking students; just the opposite of Columbia. I wonder if one still has to send a picture along with the applications?"

He let her prattle unimpeded while a few blocks passed, then spoke sharply. "There's a parking spot. On the right."

She pulled into it. "Are we there? Where?"

"At a shop called Friendly Computers," he replied, striding purposefully across the street.

"Friendly computers? What kind are those?"

"We're about to find out, Martha. Please do not become a traffic statistic." And he took her elbow and maneuvered her into the doorway of the shop.

The little shop was filled with magazines and television screens, which Liz had once told her mother were properly called cathode ray tubes. The walls were tacked with bright posters and diagrams, all meaningless to Martha's uneducated eye. The place gave forth an air of sophisticated clutter. Behind the single counter a young man sat, holding what appeared to be a walkie-talkie. As she glanced at this fellow, something prodded her in the ankle. It was a toy race car. She lifted her foot out of the way and the little thing nudged obstinately against her other ankle. It seemed to be alone.

"Want to try?" The young man smiled at her.

"To work the car?" she asked incredulously. "I can't. I never could. Machines."

He held the box under her nose. "Say 'forward.' "

"Forward?"

"Again, without the inflection."

"Forward," said Martha Macnamara. Then the words "right," "left," "stop" and "reverse" were elicited from her. Finally he placed the box in her hands.

"Now what?"

The young man beamed with pride. He was blond. Good looking. Probably a Stanford student. "Now you tell the unit what you want the car to do."

Martha knew she was the butt of a joke. She waited for the laughter to start. She glanced at Mayland Long, who watched her with noncommittal interest. No one would dare shove a walkie-talkie at *him* and tell him to say "forward," "right," "left," "stop," and reverse." A shame, too. Probably do him good.

She cleared her throat. "Turn right," she commanded. The car sat.

"Perhaps it has to be moving, before it can turn," suggested Mr. Long.

She tried, "Go forward." The tiny vehicle trundled across the carpeting and butted itself against the leg of a table.

"Far out!" she cried with instant enthusiasm. "Oh wonderful!" She commanded a right turn, a left, and then produced series of jolting jerks reminiscent of her encounters with the Mercury's clutch. In fascination, she withdrew to a chair placed before a multi-colored terminal display, where she continued her monologue of limited vocabulary.

Mayland Long turned to the shopman. "Modistics?" he inquired.

"Mostly. I took the i.d. plate off the box because I made some changes inside. How'd you guess?"

The older man shrugged his shoulders. "I have seen it advertised."

"Oh? *Byte* or *Kilobaud?*" The young man's eyes were calipers. He judged his customer closely, according to criteria known only to himself.

"Both," answered Mr. Long. "But that was in the May issues. I remember reading that the speech recognition response was inadequate. That it was easily confused by labials, in fact."

A fat man in a white shirt walked through the door. He ignored Martha and her car and they ignored him. He proceeded to the magazine rack, where he planted himself.

"S'true. I made mods. Added a laser-cut filter, and a routine to cancel noise. Least mean squares."

"You are Fred Frisch?"

He had a sizable blond moustache. He pulled on it now. "Yeah. Have I met you somewhere?"

"No. But I have met you." Mayland Long's well-tuned voice slid from polite impersonality to something a shade warmer. He lounged against the counter. "In the pages of *Dr. Dobb's*. Your article on financial system for the home computer, with a sample 8080 implementation. Interesting! Almost wasted, really, such elegant algorythms for a 16 K machine . . ."

Mr. Frisch responded to this praise. He straightened. His silky moustache whuffed. His hands worried a black power cable into circles on the dusty counter. "Did you try it?"

Long's eyes shifted only slightly. "Alas, I don't have CPM," he demurred. The fat man by the magazine rack dropped a well-thumbed copy of *Byte* back into its slot, sighing deeply.

"Oh. Well. There's that," Frisch admitted. "Interrupts would have made it run quicker, but so many people have CPM."

"You went to Stanford, I imagine," said Mayland Long, as he stared down at the floor, where the toy car was careening in circles around his legs. Martha Macnamara showed quite a skill.

"How'd you know? It wasn't in the article, was it?" asked Frisch. Immediately he answered his own question. "No. They print only your name and address: no biography. I remember that because I got letters for months after, wanting me to send free tapes."

"But you acknowleged the assistance of a Professor Carlo Peccolo for certain of your ideas. And Professor Peccolo has published in *EDN*, where a biography *did* accompany his article. How would you have received his help if you were not a student of his? Since he teaches at Stanford, it must be that . . ."

Fred Frisch cut in. "Oh sure. I see now. I thought for a moment you did auras, or like that."

Mr. Long let his toe down upon the hood of the irritating race car, which protested like an angry bee.

"But I suppose Liz Macnamara might have told me who you were, without my chance reading."

He shot a look upward and locked eyes with Frisch. "How'd you know I know Liz?"

"You were in the same department. You are of an age."

"Who are you?" countered Frisch. "You work with Liz?"

"No." He slipped his hand into his upper jacket pocket, as though to produce a card. Failing to find one, he patted the two side pocket, while furrowing his brow. Finally he spoke again. "Forgive me. My name is Long: Mayland Long. I know very little about Miss Macnamara. I am trying to learn more."

"You're a headhunter?" Fred Frisch spoke with the politeness of contempt. Mr. Long exposed his large straight teeth in a laugh.

"A job recruiter? No. Hardly. I represent a more personal interest." His voice dropped almost to a whisper. "The lady with the talent for driving is Elizabeth Macnamara's mother."

Frisch peered covertly at the top of Martha's head and at her obliviously hunched shoulders. The control box dangled unnoticed from her wrist, for she had discovered the more adult fascination of computer checkers.

"Why doesn't she ask her daughter herself?" he muttered uneasily. "I hardly know Liz."

"Elizabeth has disappeared, Mr. Frisch."

Frisch blinked at the word. "Disappeared? Jeez."

"Mrs. Macnamara lives in New York, and so she's slipped out of touch with Liz, who seems to have quit her job and moved from her last known address. We do not know who her friends are."

"I'm not the one to ask," said Frisch, for Long's ears only. "Liz's a bit of a pushin' baby, if you know what I mean."

Dryly, Mayland Long admitted he did not. "I've gathered the impression that Miss Macnamara is a rather ambitious young woman and she keeps to herself. Is that what it is to be 'a bit pushin' baby?'"

Frisch sighed and shrugged, with a half-smile that was

one-quarter apology. "Not quite. She can be friendly when she wants to. When she thinks a guy might be . . . good for her career. She got along with Peccolo."

Mr. Long's eyes widened. Frisch hurried to explain "She was his T.A.—teaching assistant, you know? They were very chummy, for a while. But it didn't last."

"Why not?"

The blond fished with one hand til he snagged the back of a high stool and pulled it under him. Once seated, he remained in thought for a count of five. "I think it was this way. Liz wants to be a manipulator—the kind who controls. Peccolo *is* that kind. Much better at it. He used her when it was supposed to be the other way around. She put in a lot of hours on the machine for him—designing his lessons, cleaning up his math . . . Peccolo is a good teacher, fine organizer—all that jazz . . ." Frisch, who had been talking to the glass counter top, suddenly sought out the other's eye. "But Liz has the technical brain. She's real good." The gaze slid away again. "Too bad technique ain't everything."

The dark man smiled slowly. His fingers drummed on the glass. "You've knocked heads with her? Don't worry about offending me; I've never met the young lady."

Frisch shuffled in place, embarrassed. "Well—no. Not me. I avoided Liz, you see, so I wouldn't."

"Do you think Peccolo would know where she is now?"

Fred Frisch shrugged once again. "Better than I," he said. "What's your part in this. Detective?"

Mayland Long laughed. Martha looked up. "Worse and worse! I'd rather be a headhunter!"

Frisch looked unconvinced.

"Mrs. Macnamara doesn't speak the jargon, you see, and my field is languages." Long found Martha standing beside him. Gently he took the controls of the racer from her hand and returned the box to Frisch.

"That fellow went to Stanford, didn't he?" asked Martha, as she was propelled across the busy street.

Mayland Long, in a graceful inversion of traditional politeness, waited for her to let herself in the driver's side, then swung around the front of the car and waited for her to reach over and unlock his door.

"So you were listening?" he replied, once in the quiet of the closed car.

"Oh no. I heard you say 'modistics' and immediately tuned out the conversation, since I would not be able to understand a word. I knew the fellow was from Stanford because he was blond, and there was a bicycle locked to the post outside." Her voice trailed off. She was thinking of something.

"Well, however you came upon it, the supposition is correct. He is a Stanford alumnus, and knows your daughter slightly."

Martha nodded. "Only slightly?"

"He has given us another name. Perhaps a more important one. Back to campus," he commanded, and the car lurched obediently forward.

"Mayland—" she began, as she found a space in the flow of traffic, entered and took it with unexpected competence. "I enjoyed myself back there. I think I missed my calling in life."

The dark man smiled and his arm, braced against the dash, relaxed to the seat. "You should have been a computer engineer?"

"Sweet Jesus, no! I should have sold toys."

4

"I'm sorry. I haven't the least idea," said the professor. He leaned back in his leather chair until the springs creaked; his pale fingers drummed against the mahogany desktop. It appeared that the conversation was over early.

Martha frowned. Her blue china eyes shone like beads. Mr. Long and she had spent the last half hour being wonderfully lost among the Spanish red sandstone buildings and the dusty live oaks of Stanford campus. They had stopped to nose into the chapel, with its gold murals and gaudy, loud, Victorian glass, and had known the satisfaction of excoriating the place together. Now it was getting hot and she was tired. Peccolo's attitude was no help.

Mayland Long drew breath slowly and spoke. "I believe she assisted you in your researches until quite recently . . ." His calm had an edge on it—an edge which told Martha she had better bite her tongue and leave this matter to him. It spoke another message to Dr. Peccolo.

"Recently? No. Not at all. She's been gone almost two years, now." He pulled himself erect again and focused over the expanse of the desk at Mr. Long. Dr. Peccolo was a much heavier man than the Eurasian, fair and stocky.

"Let me tell you something about graduate students, Mr.—uh—Long. By the way, are you in the legal profession?"

The answer was dry. "Not exactly."

"Graduate students. They come and go. Very fast. MS is two year's work. A doctorate . . . well, Elizabeth Macnamara was not headed for the doctoral program. She worked for me: grading papers, coding, handling technical correspondence. I've had two students—one per year—in that position since she graduated. No reason I should keep in touch. I'm sorry."

The last two words alone were addressed to Martha Macnamara, who sat to one side of the two men, between a wooden table piled high with printouts and a neat glass case containing, among other objects of interest, a diploma from Massachusetts Institute of

Technology, a certificate of merit from Advanced Micro Devices, and a gold urn on a marble base with the words DENVER INVITATIONAL 1959 engraved upon the side. She burned with the desire to know what sort of invitation Dr. Peccolo had received from Denver in 1959. She heard his words only distantly.

Mayland Long did not allow the interview to slip from him. "Liz Macnamara was one of the more useful finds among this flowing river of students, was she not?"

Color deepened in the professor's flat face and the muscles along his jaw gained sudden prominence. "Just how do you mean that?" he growled. His right hand plucked up a rapidograph pen and closed to a tight fist around it.

Mayland Long retained advantages of pigment and breeding. If this sudden confrontation roused him in any way it was not for the world to know. "I had heard that Miss Macnamara was quite an apt student. And diligent. Not all apprentices are like that, unless things have changed since I was young."

"She was quite competent for the sort of work I had her doing," admitted Dr. Peccolo, with no great grace. "Which was, as I told you, coding and correspondence. She had marketable skills—at least marketable today, in a society where demand has outstripped the supply of technical expertise, in a computer ghetto like the Santa Clara Valley . . . I helped her to develop these skills, and I paid her while I did so. I helped her find her first job, with Floyd Rasmussen at FSS, and I advised her against leaving it, when she came to me for advice. She has no cause for complaint."

Mayland Long regarded him abstractly. "The young woman is not complaining," he reminded the professor. "She is missing. So she came to you for advice, before leaving FSS?"

Dr. Peccolo nodded once. "It was the last time I heard from her. Over a year ago. She had this idea of going into consultant work. I told her you don't consult until people are banging on your door. Until you have a reputation."

"You consult, I imagine, professor."

"I have a reputation."

Mr. Long folded his hands amicably. "Her talents were nothing special, then?"

Dr. Peccolo stood up, nearly tipping his chair backwards. "I'm sure we are all rather special," he stated. "To our mothers."

Martha stood also, thrusting herself out of her chair with her arms. Slowly she raised her hands to her hips and faced him in this manner. She smiled at the professor who loomed over her. She began to laugh.

"I know how irritating Liz can be," she said at last. "But you shouldn't have let her get to you this way. Envy makes big men look so silly."

Mr. Long was still seated, part of his face hidden by the church steeple of his fingertips touching together in front of his mouth. He watched with interest, perhaps with amusement, as Dr. Peccolo took two steps away from Martha Macnamara's mirth and flailed behind to catch the falling chair.

As Martha sailed out the office door, Mayland Long rose sinuously to his feet, not touching the arms of the chair. His eyes were caught briefly by the angry glare of Peccolo's, but slid off toward the diploma case. "Denver, 1959," he mused. "Chess?"

The answer was grudging. "Softball."

Mr. Long nodded, thanked the professor for his time, and closed the door quietly behind him.

"Isn't this interesting?" Martha peered owlishly around her at the table of tinned biscuits, the hand-painted linen clan map of Scotland, and the black maw of the fireplace, which emitted a pleasant cold draft into the room. "The London Tea House. Actually it reminds me more of Kent. What do you think?"

Mayland Long's scrutiny was more circumspect. "I have no objections. Kent will do. Or Sussex. It might even pass for Cornwall. Any shire, borough, or city except London might have germinated such a flower as this."

Outside the row of glass doors the California sun was shining on tiered pots of geraniums. A young woman passed, wearing a light cotton pinafore and sandals. An immaculate blond toddler clung to her hand. Light from the windows of the passing cars flashed and glinted on the walls in the tea shop. Observing the street outside, Martha thought not of England, but of the Italian Riviera, which she knew only through pictures. Her gaze slid to her companion.

His improbable hands were cupped in the air before him. They steamed. Martha Macnamara was not surprised, for she had seen the blue-patterned Royal Doulton teacup disappear into his clutch.

She was tired and a little depressed, and so felt it incumbent upon her to cheer up Mr. Long. She grasped her own bottle of stout around the neck and held it up. "See that?" She pointed at the tiny, intricate harp on the label. "The original is about 750 years old. It lives at Trinity College in Dublin."

"I see." Mr. Long spoke mildly, but his forehead pulled into faint wrinkles and his eyes hooded over. He sighed before he spoke.

"My dear lady," he began. "I'm sorry our soundings this morning have not been . . . productive."

Her eyes widened in opposition to his. "Speak the truth with me, please. They have been very productive. Merely not reassuring."

"We haven't found your daughter. In fact, we have run out of leads."

"We have some history, Mayland! We know she intended to consult—go freelance. We have found two people who have been involved with Liz—one still involved enough to be touchy. In fact . . ." Here Martha raised her head to heaven. She was a vision in blue with rosy cheeks. ". . . if we only had Carlo Peccolo tied in that pig skin chair of his, and one hot poker apiece . . ."

Long grinned, showing his teeth. "Then how would we dispose of him? We couldn't very well let him go, and I, for one, have lost my taste for long pig. Still, I agree that Dr. Peccolo is a well of information not wholly emptied." He regarded his cup a while, as though it were the well in question.

"No matter. There are other ways to go about things." He raised his hands to his mouth and drained the cup.

In this action, his eyes were lowered, his face half hidden. Martha watched and she saw the West melt away from him in the simple intentness of tea. She reminded herself that this man had no business to be here with her this day, engaged in tedious toil, fencing words with unamiable people, measuring miles of hot pavement in search of a young woman he probably had no interest to meet.

She remembered further, distantly, as though out of a story read in childhood, that Mayland Long was a rich man.

She shook her head in dismissal. He told wonderful stories in a wonderful voice. That was far more important. He tended to drowse in the light of the sun—she had seen that twice today: once by the window of his apartment, and once in the car. She recalled his words—"I have always respected warmth and the ability to keep still." Perhaps he was drowsing now, behind the empty cup, as his elbows rested on the table and the quiet of mid-afternoon filled the shop. He was a man. He got tired. He could be hurt. She thought about that last one: he could be hurt.

Suddenly the spectre of parting sprang up her mind, forbidding as the shadow of an axe. She started, and the brown eyes caught her motion. He had not been asleep.

Martha spoke. "I will be concerned when I can do something about this. When my concern will be useful. And I *will* reach that point. I'm going to find Liz."

He nodded, accepting her certainty. "Perhaps it's time for the police to help."

"No. Not yet. I don't feel that." She pursed her

mouth, seeking the words for explanation. She raised her glass and took a long swallow of the black beer. "You see, Liz has never feared God or the devil. When she says she might be in trouble, well, I don't know with whom. God or the devil."

"Are the police one of the above?" he inquired, bringing one arm up to rest along the chairback. "Would she have called you into the mess if she were in trouble with the law?"

"I doubt it, Mayland. But I've got another reason for hesitating." Martha frowned, trying to explain. "When Liz was nine she was picked up on Riverside Drive by a policeman who thought she looked lost. She wasn't, of course; we lived in a building right around the corner on West 106th. But Liz didn't tell him that. She thought it was none of his business. She spent three hours in the station and never told them who she was or where she lived. Complete stonewall, and just because she was angry. And she didn't call me, either, though the officers would have been glad to let her use the phone—I only found out about it when she didn't come home for dinner and I called the police. That's the kind of person she is.

"Liz's held a grudge against blue uniforms ever since. She wouldn't thank me if I reported her missing."

Long shrugged. His suit jacket rustled, dry as paper. "Then our next step must be to question Floyd Rasmussen of FSS. He may know something about this consultant work she planned."

"I'm going to do that in the morning," Martha said, rummaging in her purse. "Perhaps I can arrange to meet him for lunch."

"It might be easier if I call, arranging the meeting on some technical pretext." He broached the subject warily.

The large floral purse shut with a snap. "No, Mayland. I think you'd better not go any deeper into this."

The dark face drew back. The long hands flattened on the table. "I admit I have intruded into affairs which are not my business, my dear . . . Martha. But you've convinced me there's an element of danger in this."

Her head bobbed forcefully. The gray braid threatened to slide. "Yes. That's exactly why I want you out of it."

His expression went blank—as blank as it had been when she teased him about the word "Oolong." Then Mayland Long laughed, a low rumble which ran along the walls of the room, echoed in corners and tangled among the legs of the wooden chairs. The cashier in the corner raised her head. When the laughter subsided, a wide smile remained.

"You are concerned about me? About my respectability perhaps? My personal safety?"

Martha Macnamara's nostrils flared. She thumped her bag heavily. "Why not? Are you superman? Do you know everything?"

The smile faded. "No. I am not. I do not. I am only Mayland Long, and as I have said before you must tell me what I am to do, and how I am to live my life properly."

She looked sideways at him, waiting for the punchline.

"Shall I go back to my rooms in the James Herald Hotel and sit there with the pot and the kettle, many books and a bronze dragon, stepping out only to visit Barnes and Noble, and to dine on white linen in the Crystal Room?"

She opened her mouth but did not speak.

"I'll tell you plainly, Martha, I came to San Francisco waiting for something to happen. Something that was—predicted—for me years ago in Taipei. A sign. An awakening. It is rank superstition on my part to believe in this, perhaps, but as a result of this prophecy I have changed my living, my language, my . . ." His words died away and his fingers drummed the table top. "I have changed in many ways." His eyes met hers briefly, then slid away. "It is hard to change when one is old. It's almost easier to give up and die. Almost."

"Do you know how to give up?" asked Martha quietly.

"No." He smiled ruefully and his eyebrows rose like wings. "Is that something I must learn?"

He gave her no time to reply. "But you mustn't expect me to behave like a Westerner, Martha, just because I speak the language. Nor like a . . . man of the present."

Martha leaned forward, peering left and right in conspiritorial fashion, wearing a small, round, Buddha-smile. "My dear Mr. Long," she whispered, "I expect everything and nothing of you. And I wouldn't be surprised if you rose from this table and flew off among the hanging geraniums. I would assume you had a reason.

"And I assume you had a reason to come to San Francisco, and a reason to park yourself at the James Herald. If you came on the strength of a prophecy, well then, you're working with clearer goals than most people."

She drew back an inch, but her gaze didn't waver. "What are you seeking?"

Mayland Long lifted his head and as he spoke the light struck his face, turning his eyes oak yellow. "Among other things—truth."

"Among other things!" Martha folded her hands. "What else is there?"

He mimicked her gesture, laughing. "Don't ask me such a question! I have never been good with paradox. Isn't it enough for you that I've revealed the core of superstition that lies at the heart of this man in a business suit? But I will share with you a thing I have learned—that I am learning even now. I discover that waiting may be accomplished in divers ways. And stillness has many . . . appearances, as does warmth. Your own sort of stillness, for instance, Martha, can be full of movement, like a tree full of birds. Yet I see it as stillness. And your warmth . . . Well, that is marvelous, like the color of your eyes."

She exclaimed involuntarily. "My eyes? Marvelous?"

"Certainly. Blue is a cold color, yet the brighter the

sun shines, the more blue is the sky." He paused, regarding her blue eyes, her blushing face.

"Martha, I am through sitting passive. Realization is not a dove to be coaxed to the hand. It will find one or it will not.

"Besides—what if my chance for understanding has come and gone, unrecognized? What if signs and events of all colors and meaning: joys, sorrows, wonderments— have passed by and are lost because I have been too busy looking for a box with the label 'truth' on it? I want to help you find Elizabeth—not because I am altruistic, but because I am curious and alone. I like puzzles and I enjoy your company. I think I can be useful, if you will allow me to be."

She put her hands to the sides of her round head. "I don't understand half what you're saying. And what can I answer? You're using my own arguments against me!"

He shrugged, and the fabric of his suit jacket rustled dryly. It was silk. "You can agree to a collaboration. Together we will find your daughter."

She touched his hand.

Martha parked in a lot a quarter mile away from the hotel, where the parking was cheaper. They began walking.

San Francisco was ten degrees cooler than the peninsula, though the same dry, Italianate sun shone. A large gull flew past them along Van Ness, strafing the cars. Having just crossed Turk Street, Mayland Long spied something on the sidewalk and bent to pick it up.

It was a red rose bud, its petals disarranged, the stem half torn through where a pin had pulled out. He grunted and smoothed it out as though it were wrinkled cloth. "The rose," he announced. "Loveliest and most formidible of flowers. Arms of York and Lancaster. In medieval times, symbol of Jesus. Always, it has meant, beauty, love, peace . . ."

He presented the bud to Martha Macnamara. It lay

resting on his long fingers until she scooped it up. She sniffed it and held it up in the light.

"Symbol? What's a symbol? This is a rose." She smiled and walked on.

The moment rang for Mayland Long—rang as though the entire sky had become a gong and Martha Macnamara had struck it. He stood still, while the gray stone city reeled about him.

The four words echoed in his head. "This is a rose." The simple, dumb truth of them announced the universe.

And he stood there for an endless moment—perhaps two or three seconds by the clock—a thin man in a dark suit, rather old, rather elegant, rather frail, rubbing his thumb along the length of his hand and feeling the memory of a rose.

Then he moved quickly, his eye fixed on the receding blue dress. She knew who he was. She had shown him his own face, reflected in all creation. But did she know who *she* was? Standing alone and perfect, or standing by him—did she know what she was to him? He snaked forward along the crowded street, burning with a desire to tell her.

Martha Macnamara reached the corner just as the walk sign lit. She did not seem to realize she had left her companion behind, nor that she had redeemed his life. She stepped into the street. A bus pulled into the crosswalk behind her, concealing her from Mayland Long's sight. A black Lincoln stopped at the corner parallel to her path, then turned right into the crosswalk.

The light changed as Mr. Long reached the corner. He raised his eyes over the roofs of the cars, seeking the blue dress along the next block.

She was not there. Martha Macnamara was nowhere along the street between Mayland Long and the James Herald Hotel. Nor was she in the lobby.

Nor in her room.

She was gone.

5

The early sun pried silently into the window. It counted the books in Mayland Long's sitting room. The black statue against the side wall drank in the sun's light, reflecting it only through the eyes.

One of the two armchairs in the room had been turned toward the bare window; the chair was dull gold. So was the skin of the man asleep in that chair, his head resting in the angle of the wing-back. The dark silk suit-jacket he had worn the day before was thrown across the chair arm; one empty sleeve dragged upon the wooden floor.

In sleep, Mr. Long's strange hands and features asked no explanations. They merely were: facts of nature like tangled tree roots, like the face of a tiger, like the odd, water-washed stones on the cold beach visible from his high window.

The edge of bright light finished with the bookshelf and crawled across the carpet to the chair. It touched his face and hands, and the sleeping man relaxed into it. His head slipped against the fabric and his eyes cracked open to receive the dazzle of sunlight. He blinked. Yawned. Twisted left and right in the chair. Finally he peered behind him at the still, uncluttered room, as though it could tell him why he found himself in the sitting room, fully dressed.

Then he remembered, and with the arrival of memory his hands groped for the chair arms. The padded wood protested with small creaks.

Yesterday evening had been the phone call to the San Francisco police. The polite, endlessly repeated explanation of who he was, who Martha Macnamara was, and why he believed she had met foul play. He had not told them all he knew, because it had been necessary to balance his concern—no, give it its true name—his *fear* for Martha against the woman's own determination not to involve her daughter with the police. He could only repeat that Mrs. Macnamara had been walking along Van Ness with him, and had vanished at the corner of Fell Street. That she had not yet returned to her room, though she was still registered at the James Herald Hotel, that the desk clerk had not seen her.

That she had been worried about something.

It was hardly a compelling story. It carried the implication that Mrs. Macnamara had dropped out of sight to avoid him, and his call to the authorities further intimated that he was the sort of importunate busybody a person might well want to avoid.

The officer had told him that they would have to wait at least a day before they could regard the woman as missing. The policeman had taken down name and address.

He had realized the uselessness of the attempt then, and had tried no further to interest the police. He knew the disparity between his voice and person; if his words could not convince, then his face and form would be of no help.

Besides, if Martha Macnamara had been killed by whoever it was who snatched her up—no one in the bus, surely. The black Lincoln?—then she *was* dead, and neither police nor power could bring her back.

And if she was alive, spirited away somewhere, then she was kept alive for a purpose, and would doubtless remain that way until the purpose was fulfilled. In that case, the police were still not much help, but another power might be. Without conscious arrogance Mayland Long applied that title to himself. Another power.

And he was sure with a granite certainty that Martha Macnamara was not dead. He would know if she were.

For if she were dead, then hope was dead, and his own existence turned to ashes.

And, looking at the gray, waking city, the quiet mirror of the bay, the jangled mirror of the sea, he did not feel dead nor burnt out. He felt—he turned the unfamiliar emotion over in his mind with intellectual curiosity, trying to identify it—he felt angry.

He rose from the chair and brushed at the crumpled jacket without seeing it. He was trying to remember the last time he had felt anger. Three years in San Francisco. One in Kyoto. Before that, Taipei—two years. There came grief and loss. Even fear. Anger? No. No one to be angry at, that evening in Taipei. Not even himself.

And before Taipei there had been no need at all for anger.

He stopped this raking of memory. No need. He knew what anger was. It was hot.

Like Carlo Peccolo, Floyd Rasmussen was a fair, stocky man, but there the resemblance ended. Peccolo kept his credentials under glass, while Rasmussen had a wall stuck full of clippings from the Sunday funnies, along with three Kliban cats. Peccolo was sober, but Rasmussen laughed. He rattled the windows with his laughter. He laughed when Long introduced himself. He chuckled at the name of Dr. Peccolo. He let loose gales of laughter when Mr. Long brought forward the subject of Liz Macnamara, and with his wiry yellow beard and wiry yellow hair spreading out from his face, Floyd Rasmussen was the image of some Aztec sun god, graved in gold.

"Liz? She's done work for me. I hope she will again, though the money she's asking now . . . Oh Lord, yes, I know Liz Macnamara. That's like asking me how well I know Blanco, my cat. Liz is a warrior, bright, spunky, ambitious. She brought life to RasTech . . ."

Coolly Mayland Long wondered how much more life

the company called RasTech could bear. Floyd Rasmussen seemed to fill all available corners with his own vital substance. Mr. Long pulled at the tiller of the conversation.

"Bright? Then you would say her level of technical ability was above average?"

"Average? You can hardly use that word in the same breath as Liz Macnamara. She's original. Sound. Big systems, little systems, software, firmware, pc layout . . . Just give her a handful of bipolar vlsi chips and stand back. She can even, occasionally, meet a deadline. And I don't say that for most of my friends!"

This last admission dissolved into dull rumbles. Floyd Rasmussen beamed at Mr. Long.

The office did not contain a desk. Rasmussen worked from a drafting table set against one wall. There was thus no barrier between the booming geniality of the president of RasTech and the fastidious composure of his guest. Mayland Long did not feel that the advantage was his.

"Then, it was not out of line for her to set herself up as a consultant—to go free-lance?"

The big man snorted. "What else should she do? Give half her salary for a benefits package and insurance, and the other half to Uncle Sugar? She's gone the smart way, consulting."

Long prodded patiently. "Even at her age, without contacts? Dr. Peccolo believed . . ."

". . . in Santa Claus. He doesn't like knowing a young whippersnapper he was supposed to be teaching actually had more on the ball than he did." Rasmussen's furry eyebrows pulled together and his mouth pursed.

"Carlo's a friend of mine. Hurts me to say it, but he's not that good, technically." His voice expressed no great pain.

Mayland Long digested this—both the words and the manner. "Tell me, Mr. Rasmussen. Just what did Elizabeth Macnamara do for you at FSS which convinced you to hire her services here, in your own company?"

"Eh?" Rasmussen stopped to think. A few moments of silence leaked into the office.

"She did lots of things. An interface board for teller's terminals: Z80 based. An accounts receivable package in 6502 assembler. Half a bank security system . . ."

"Half a bank security system?"

Rasmussen grunted and shrugged. "We only got the contract for half. Works that way a lot. Maybe their guy quits in the middle of the job and they don't want to train a programmer from scratch, or . . . Well, lots of things. Then, let's see—she wrote a disk controller for our own use." Rasmussen stopped. He crinkled little eyes behind sandy lashes. It was difficult to tell what color those eyes were.

" 'Zat the kind of thing you want to know?"

Mayland Long detached his gaze from the man and swept it once around the square, unsubtle room. One wall was orange; that was the one dotted with comic clippings. One wall was stenciled with a single, diagonal black stripe, dipping left. Against that wall stood a model of a sailing boat, white, gleaming, intricate, its spiky rigging echoed in the tines of a set of deer antlers hung above. The carpet was looped in orange and green. The plastic chair he sat on was yellow.

Mayland Long, in his quiet gray suit, felt like a quote taken out of context.

"Yes, Mr. Rasmussen, that is part of it. And, since you do not have a current address or phone number for the lady, I shall have to be satisfied with that much." He rose to his feet.

Rasmussen heaved his own bulk off the drafting stool. "She'll call me once she's settled in her new place. It always takes a month or so to let people know when you've moved. That's a real problem when you're self-employed. I know. Been there."

He reached out to shake Mayland Long's hand. Shaking hands was a ritual Floyd Rasmussen practiced whenever he could, and somehow his guest had begun their conversation without it. He succeeded in grabbing Long's unresisting hand now, but there was something wrong in the gesture. This was not the usual wrongness which accompanies shaking hands: cold, wet palm, no strength in the grip, or too much. The hand he commandeered was dry and warm. It held his own securely, without squeezing the knuckles together. The wrongness was in the shape of it.

He dropped his eyes from the dusky face, but the hand had been withdrawn. Mayland Long was speaking.

"You have not asked what my interest is in Miss Macnamara. Aren't you curious?"

Rasmussen looked up in surprise. "Your interest? You're looking to use her, right? But you weren't sure she was the engineer you needed. Peccola gave her sort of a lukewarm recommendation and you wanted a second opinion?"

Mayland Long smiled. It was not an English smile, but a Chinese smile. "Very close. I have need of her, and am interested to know what she has been doing. I worry I may not find her in time." He turned to leave.

"Well, I wouldn't worry," boomed Rasmussen down the hall. "Don't . . . commit yourself to anything yet. She'll show."

Mr. Long found himself on Mathilda avenue, feeling the even, flat, shadeless street and the reek of traffic as a relief after the force of Rasmussen's joviality. He fingered the keys of his own car, a small green Citroën. He sifted among Rasmussen's words. Gold and dross: how to tell one from the other? Turning the ignition key, his face meditative, he felt for the anger he had found within himself earlier.

It was still present, and it retained the same size and shape. Good. If he was to be angry, Mayland Long wanted that anger to de dependable.

* * *

Today there was no buzzing robot-car on the floor of Friendly Computers. Instead, Fred Frisch was involved in a lengthy discussion with a boy who appeared both too young and too poor to have business there. The subject of the dialogue was breadboards, a large assortment of which lay scattered across the counter. At least half the display machines along the wall were running, some throwing fantasies of color over their screens, while others flashed words. One unit emitted a monotonous beep, beep, beep as images of tiny rockets exploded into flame.

Mr. Long did not attempt to interrupt the conversation, but sat down in the same chair that Martha Macnamara had graced the previous morning. The repetitive, multi color display on the nearest video screen caught his interest. Mayland Long's experience with computing was as extensive as the books in his library and existed on no other level. He pressed the return key tentatively.

The display vanished, leaving in its place a list of available games and instructions for invoking them. He conjured up something called simply *Life*.

The resultant display was impressive. Small cells of white grew over the screen from dots of his placing. These expanded like lichen, and like lichen died away in the middle. Mr. Long grasped the mathematics of it, and also the metaphor. His eyes watched tiny colonies grow, proliferate, compete with one another for space, fail through mysterious inner processes, die . . . Like societies of men.

It was a game he was quite familiar with, watching mankind from a distance: civilizations, tribes, individuals . . . As always, he felt a desire to interfere.

He focused on one white speck, no different from any of its fellows. It was one of the rare stable ones, situated in a small pulsing colony. It might continue forever, or at least until the next power failure.

But wait—no. At the far edge of the screen a small, odd-shaped colony was moving sideways. A glider. It left the screen at the right and re-entered from the far left. Its path was going to impact the pulsar in . . . how many moves?

Mayland Long worked the puzzle in his mind. He saw each move that would bring the attacker toward the small colony. He constructed the impact, and saw in foresight the end of that tiny dot of light, no different from any other on the screen.

He sat motionless and watched, his eyes black, his face impassive. But a moment before the glider intersected the stable colony, his hand struck the keyboard of the computer, freezing the action.

"Live," he whispered to the dot of light.

He heard movement behind him. Frisch stood there, dangling a green plastic board from his nervous hands. "Ever play that before?" he asked. "*Life?*"

Long looked around him at the empty store. "Not this . . . implementation."

"I suppose everyone's got one," the young man admitted. "But this one's faster. Most of them are written in BASIC. Would you believe that?"

Long did not answer. He stretched out an arm, found another plastic tub chair and pulled it into position beside his own.

Obediently, Frisch sat. "You haven't found her, I guess."

Mayland Long smiled ruefully. "Progress has been retrograde. I have now lost the mother."

Frisch stared. "Maybe she gave up and went home."

"If she did, she left her luggage behind." Long's gesture made circles in the air.

"Mr. Frisch . . ."

"Fred."

"Will you answer me a few more questions? I realize you're busy and I'm a bother . . ."

Frisch bit his lower lip and pulled on his moustache. "I'm not busy," he admitted. "And I don't mind talking. But as I said yesterday, I don't really know Liz."

"These are technical questions. You see, I value the

breadth of your interest. You understand both methodology and personality. I imagine you know Floyd Rasmussen."

"RasTech," answered Frisch promptly, responding to the flattery with innocent eagerness. "I don't *know* him, though. Just about him."

"Go on, please. I know him, you see, but do not know about him."

The young shopowner took a deep breath. "Rasmussen. He's a mover. Sharp. Not a technical man, but a great entrepreneur. He's made a lot of money."

"On his own?"

Frisch nodded affirmation. "He's started half-a-dozen firms in the last ten years."

"Then why was he working for FSS in the position of department manager last year?"

"Oh, he's lost a lot of money, too. His last couple of ideas went bust: small business systems." Frisch began intensive demolition work upon his moustache, his eyes puckered, staring through the blank window of his shop at the street beyond.

"But I don't think he was personally hurt either time—just the stockholders. Only I imagine it's hard to find any more capital after two Chapter Elevens."

"Evidently he has managed," interjected Mr. Long. He sighed and murmured, "Interesting.

"Tell me . . . Fred. Why would a bank want to hire an engineer to write half a security system?"

There was no hesitation in Fred's reply. "So the right hand won't know what the left hand is doing. It's often done that way. Like for the little plastic cards they use nowadays. You know? Supposedly no one knows the algorithm by which the card code is evolved out of the account number, or the customer's name. That's because two programmers wrote it. Each knows half.

"A bank'll go to a lot of trouble to randomize the choice, hiring one man on this end of the country and one in New York, taking two or even three programmers out of different segments of the field—industry, research, schools."

"Have you ever been involved in such a project, Fred?"

"No, not me." He shook his head, releasing his moustache from its duress. "That's big league stuff. They don't look for a hacker with his head full of new ideas and his heart among the hobbyists."

Frisch frowned as he spoke, but his eyes remained vague, reflecting the sky through the window: detached, speculative, feeling his grievances against the world only superficially. He was very young. Mayland Long found him interesting. His own brown eyes, watching Frisch, were anything but vague.

"But Peccolo has done security. He contracted for one while I was at Stanford. I remember. It was for North Bay Savings."

Long stirred in his chair. "While you were at Stanford. That must be—oh—two years ago, then? You've not done badly, being only two years out of school. This shop filled with expensive toys, contacts in all fields of electronics . . ."

Frisch linked his hands together behind his head and cracked all his knuckles at once, exhaling loudly through his moustache as he did so. "Well, I guess not. This shop? Yeah, it's something."

The young man got up and regarded the row of screens before him. Some of them were dusty. Some dotted with fingerprints. He turned to the wall of esoteric journals, and the counter filled with boxes of components, spools of bright ribbon cable, and small chips laid like dead roaches on their backs, brass legs sparkling under glass. "Seems I never sell anything, though. I just have interesting conversations."

Long laughed at Fred Frisch and then, unexpectedly, he bowed to him, hands together across his middle, thumbs lightly touching. "May you have many more such," he said, his accent shifting slightly from Oxford to the East. "And may they be of equal value to the people with which you have them."

He took his leave. As the door closed behind him, Fred Frisch leaned over to the console and hit the return key. The program resumed, the glider touched the small pulsing colony, and one particular dot of light went out.

No one saw who cared.

6

There were clouds toward the north, over the city. These darkened the rear-view mirror, while Mayland Long drove into the late afternoon sun. They reminded him that autumn was approaching: autumn and the rain.

He took a deep breath and let it out slowly. His left arm lay along the sill of the open window. His bare hand sprawled out over the dark green enamel of the car door: too dark for the sun to burn.

Fire was Mr. Long's chosen element; he had no sympathy with the rain. Yet he knew water was pre-ordained to win, in the end. In man's end, at least. No vault or sepulcher could keep out the damp forever, and even ashes dissolved. But if he stared at the mirror with a bleak eye, driving south on Alma Street in the dusty shade of trees, it was not such philosophical speculation which disturbed him.

He parked out of the line of sight of anyone coming from or going toward RasTech, and strolled down the street. Mathilda Avenue was wide and choked with traffic. The earth around it—like the entire Valley—was flat and dry, only partially won from desert. In Long's eyes it was an unworthy victory, too. The cheap concrete architecture depressed him; it seemed to spring out of nowhere, like the sudden idea of some not-very-imaginative child: all boxes and cylinders, not even colored with crayon.

Each bare-fronted building had its tiny, begrudged rectangle of green and a huge parking lot. The only other shrubbery on the street consisted of the occasional ivy bed, and a few sapling olive trees which struggled for life at the corner, where the words Sunnyvale Industrial Park were engraved on a sign cut from an immense slice out of a redwood tree. RasTech itself was featureless as a shoebox, except for heavy concrete buttresses along the side of each window and which made a sort of porch before the front entrance.

This landscape offered very little concealment to a man seeking concealment—especially a man as distinctive in appearance as Mayland Long. Nonetheless he concealed himself, standing motionless in the afternoon shadows cast by the overhang of the entrance. Behind him rose the slab wall of the building. To his left was the lintel of the doorway. In front of him, further obscuring him from sight, stood a lattice overwhelmed by mounds of Algerian ivy. His clothes were dark; so was he. The shadow slowly grew.

People issued from the building—it was nearly five o'clock. RasTech employees accounted for only a fraction of the workers who dashed out or paused on the walk before the door, expanding in the open air for a moment before confronting the traffic. Long searched them all from the darkness; his eyes were very good.

He waited for Rasmussen, knowing he might well have a long wait. He wanted information from the president of RasTech, the last known employer of Elizabeth Macnamara. He did not think he would obtain that information by asking the man. He planned to follow him.

Mayland Long was tired. Save for those few hours in the chair early in the morning, he had been awake for three days. He was also hungry, having neglected to eat since the previous day's lunch with Martha Macnamara.

He had no patience for the way his body clamored to be fed, two or even three times a day.

Sleep, however, he took seriously. He liked to sleep, and he would have to sleep tonight, or his mind would begin to fail. He told himself as much and continued his watch.

Three women came out of the door, dressed in tight trousers, talking in Spanish. He followed their conversation with half an ear. A man came out alone: too thin to be Rasmussen. Then a young woman appeared. She let the door slam behind her and stood hesitant on the stoop.

She was tall and blonde, dressed in tailored navy blue gabardine. She turned her head left and right, as though she could not remember where she had parked her car. Mayland Long took a step out of the shadow and froze.

Beneath the smooth grace of hair, above the strong jawline, she had the blue eyes of her mother. She was taller, yes. Larger of bone. Most probably Martha Macnamara had never been this beautiful.

Nor, probably, had she ever been so quietly terrified. The face Mayland Long saw in profile was white and sweating, concealing a sick fear. The perfect lips trembled. Seeing this in a reflection of Martha, whose listening had pulled from him more than he had believed himself to know, who had said, "This is a rose" and thereby cracked all the barriers in his life, his abiding anger flared. One hand clutched at the redwood grating before him. Wood crumbled.

She headed for the street, her foot stumbling once on the concrete stair. She wound through the crowded parking lot, among cars that honked and bulled their way toward the exits. She climbed the grass edgeway and was at the street.

Mayland Long followed. He abandoned the shadow, fading unnoticed through the crowd of loungers at the door. He pursued Liz Macnamara at a distance. She stopped by a white Mercedes and stepped out to the driver's side. Standing a distance away, he smiled, imagining Martha behind the wheel of that car. Then he turned back the way he had come.

She bolted the door behind her and leaned against it. Immediately the shaking grew worse. She bit her lip until she had her body in control again.

Hearing the sound of the fountain in the courtyard, she strode over to the living room window. With repeated thumps of the heel of her hand, she forced the sash open.

Cool air stole into the room, smelling of water. The pampered grass of the central court waved silver and green. There were gulls in the fountain; she heard the smack of their wings.

Liz had heard a story about geese being used to keep watch in some country; warning of invaders. Where was that—Greece? Would these gulls cry out if one of the condominiums were invaded? She peered down at the sidewalk that wound through the grass below, and at the shingles of the wall. Finally she turned away from the window.

Mumbling to herself, she pushed open the bedroom door and pulled off her suit. This she hung on a wooden hanger, with a care born out of habit. She pulled a pair of blue jeans out of the dresser drawer and put them on, along with a French T-shirt. Then she flung herself across the bed, trying to cry. Huge, painful sobs sounded for five minutes, wracking her body, while the bed dandled and rocked her. Abruptly she gave up the effort, for no matter how she wailed, her eyes remained dry. She could not cry for her mother. She could not cry for herself.

Suddenly she jackknifed from the bed. Had she heard something? For almost a minute she stood listening. But why would they want to break in on her? They knew the thing they wanted was not there. And they knew better than to touch her personally.

She sighed silently. Hysteria was no use; she had to think. She brushed her hair back with her fingers. Her hands were large boned, her arms long. The only thought that occurred to her was that she wanted a drink. Barefoot, she paced into the kitchen.

She could reach the high cupboard easily. For years mother had depended on her to fetch things like the meat chopper from the cabinet on top of the fridge. Now her fingers closed on a dusty quart bottle of Teacher's and brought it down. Setting it on the butcher-block table, she opened the china cupboard, where the tea cups hung in rows from little hooks, and picked out a pebble-bottomed tumbler. She poured and downed the shot without tasting; Liz didn't really like Scotch. She poured another and stared at it. After five minutes she capped the bottle and headed for the sink to dump the tumbler. She heard a step behind her.

The only thought she could muster was that the geese had let her down. But they weren't geese, of course. They were gulls. She swivelled and raised her slim right arm. With excellent aim, she threw the bottle of Teacher's at the sound.

And stood staring at the apparition in her kitchen: an elegant, swarthy man with black hair and a gray suit, whose hand wrapped around the sloshing bottle. Who smiled and said diffidently, "Thank you. Usually I use a glass."

Liz's lungs filled with air, but the scream never arrived. "Shit!" she cried instead. "Who the hell are you?"

He stood for a moment, brow furrowed, holding the bottle of whiskey. It was as though her question required some thought. "I am . . . not an enemy, Miss Macnamara. In fact, I am probably the best hope you have."

"Who are you?" she repeated in a small voice—a child's voice. Then stronger. Angry. "Who *are* you? Rasmussen never said . . ."

"Rasmussen? No, miss. I do not represent the interests of Floyd Rasmussen." Calmly, he set the bottle back on the table, while his eyes followed her closely.

Her hands clenched repeatedly. "Then who? Where'd

you come from? How'd you get in here?" Liz Macnamara stalked closer, stiff legged, amazement and outrage overcoming her fear.

The man, by contrast, leaned insouciantly against the table, rolling the bottle from hand to hand. "My name is Long—Mayland Long. I am sent by your mother to find you."

She took one more step forward, a cry escaping from between clenched teeth. She grabbed at Mr. Long's sleeves, caught one brown hand and held it. "Then she's all right. He lied? She's not being held . . ."

Her words slowed and stopped, as she glanced down at the dark fingers clutched in her own. She stared at the hand, puzzled.

Long sighed. "She is not all right at all. She has vanished, and if you have been told that she is being held somewhere, it is probably not a lie."

Two second's worth of hope died in the young woman's face. Without another glance at Long, she walked into the living room and sat down on the bright, chrome-framed sofa. Jaw clenching spasmodically, she stared out the window. He, meanwhile, made a quick circuit of the room, drawing the drapes. Lacy panels of fiberglass filtered the light, concealing them from the outside and casting a pattern of brilliant squares against the stark white walls. In the dimness Long was nearly invisible, but the woman's skin shone like blue glass. Wind blew the drapes about, sending the dappled wall into a star-dance.

Long sat down beside Liz Macnamara. "Elizabeth. Your mother is taken but she is not dead. We've got no time to brood."

Her eyes shocked open. She stared at the strange face so close to her own. "O hell!" she whispered. "I can't believe this is really happening."

Hers was a strong face, smooth and lean featured. A Viking face. Suppressed fury sharpened its lines. "I did this to her . . . I did."

He raised his eyebrows as he settled himself cau-

tiously into the ultramodern foam sofa. "Yes, I rather
think you did," he agreed, his voice terribly gentle.

He turned to her in the dimness, with no sound
except the rustle of silk. "You have been playing with the
big boys, Miss Macnamara."

These words pierced through Liz's funk. Her jaw
tightened and she pulled herself up. "What do you mean
by that crack? Why shouldn't I 'play with the big boys?' "

He folded his hands on his knee and considered. "No
reason at all.

"But in this particular sort of game one does not call on
one's mother when things go badly. You see?"

Liz Macnamara dropped her eyes. "You're right. How
can I explain? It felt like a nightmare, you see, and
mother was always so good with nightmares.

"My mother has the power to put perspectives
right . . . She's so—so confident. I thought nothing
nasty could touch her."

Then, abruptly, her hands clenched. "You can't know
about this. Not unless you're from them: from Rasmussen or Threve. But I don't know why they sent you.
What more can you want from me? I'll get the letter
tomorrow; the banks are already closed today."

Mayland Long drank in this assortment of information. "Your mother also shifts mood like that: floats like
dust in the air and then comes down with a great crash. I
had thought this was part of her spiritual attainment, but
perhaps she was born that way."

He met the confused stubbornness in Elizabeth's face
and sighed. He let his eyes wander through the starkly
furnished, expensive rooms.

Liz Macnamara's home was sharp angled, glacial pale.
The walls were neither ecru, dove nor cream but a white
so pure as to shimmer with blue. On the bare, bleached
oak floor were scattered cobalt Rya rugs, like holes in
smooth ice. On a table in the dining ell rested a tray of
Swedish glass, glinting smooth and colorless.

Long's brow darkened. "What can I say that will
convince you? Let's see . . . You don't get along with

your mother. She irritates you. Makes you feel vaguely guilty. You believe she has abandoned her true life's work as a concert violinist."

Her face remained frozen. "You got that from Rasmussen. I told him all that a long time ago."

He sighed, raised his hand to the side of his head, and scratched his ear with one elongated finger. Liz Macnamara stared at that finger, fascinated.

"Did you tell him also that your mother wakes every morning at five to do zazen? That she appreciates the poems of John Donne?

"That she can listen to . . . a person . . . until truth comes out of him? Sometimes it's a truth that never was truth before?"

Liz's jaw worked. She sorted the words Long spoke so diffidently. Her eyes sought reassurance in his impassive face.

"Do you even know these things about her?" His voice sank away.

There was silence in the room. Suddenly Liz Macnamara got up and paced to the window. The drapes swirled about her as she peered out at the gulls in the shower of the fountain.

"How did you get in here?"

He hesitated before answering. "Through that window."

"Here?" She leaned out. "It's ten feet from the ground," she accused. "The wall is shingle."

He sighed, as though he were being compelled to speak on a subject he found in poor taste. "Only the top six feet are shingle. The foundation is brick." He shrugged off the doubt in her eyes, obviously irritated. "Believe what you will. I'm here.

"And I'm here for a reason. As of yesterday, my goal was merely to locate you, Miss Macnamara. I promised your mother I would help her. Now you must help me find her."

Mayland Long raised himself from the couch, frowning; in the soft depths of foam his thinking was hindered.

He strode across the room and sat down in a white wicker chair. His back was straight. His fingers thrust among the twisted reeds. "It is time for you to tell me what you know," he announced.

Elizabeth Macnamara sat in the shadowed room, looking at the wall. "I've been robbing a bank."

"I guessed as much." His voice reflected a dry triumph.

Her head spun toward him. Her hair made a dim halo around her face. "You guessed? How . . . how did you? What kind of detective are you? From the police?"

The complexity of her mistake amused Long, but the woman did not see his smile. "No, miss. I'm not from the police. Your mother didn't want to call the police."

Liz settled again, but wary as a bird. "How did you find out, then? Do you know how I did it?" It was difficult to see Long in the dark. He sat very still.

"I believe I do. You wrote half of a bank securities package for North Bay Savings, while you were at FSS. What the bank did not know was that you had assisted Dr. Peccolo of Stanford to design the other half."

Liz shook her head violently. "Assisted, nothing. I wrote the whole thing. He said it would be valuable experience for me."

"Was it?" asked Mayland Long. His teeth glimmered briefly.

Elizabeth let out a shuddering groan. As she turned from Long to the window she seemed to gather the stray light around her. Outside the gulls keened.

"Shit! Lies lead from one to the other. That was Carlo's lie—that he had done the system. It was the first bit of rottenness in this whole mess. I'd been dating him almost all of my second year in grad school—on the sly, of course. He's married.

"But I broke with him while I was doing the security package. I realized he was using me, and it just stuck in my craw, you know?"

Long didn't answer. She continued. "And *how* he used me! I thought Carlo was a wizard in the beginning. My—

my mentor! He said he would take care of me, lead me to the top. I wanted to be a wizard too."

She snorted. "I was a real innocent."

"A wizard," Long echoed, thoughtfully. "Odd word to use in connection with computers. I've always found there to be so much . . . flimflam about wizards, and I can't see how one could get away with that in computer engineering. But perhaps that's my own innocence.

"At any rate, if the masters of your art are called wizards, then I'm sure you deserve the name."

She recoiled, shaking her head.

"I've heard about you from all sides, Miss Macnamara. I'm told you are very good at what you do.

"And meeting you, I now know two computer wizards." Long chuckled at his private joke.

She fought against vanity and curiosity both. "I don't know what you mean," she answered, sullen. "I told you I'm not . . ."

"I don't mean anything," Long murmured. "Go on. You never mentioned to anyone you had done Peccolo's work for him? Not even when you were so—bitter?"

"He knew." The words were a hiss. Liz took two steps toward Long's chair, placing herself between him and the fading light of the window. Though her figure was a mere silhouette against the dusk, the smugness in her voice was unmistakable. "I knew he knew. And he was never sure whether I had told anyone. I let him sweat it."

Mayland Long stirred in his chair. "A subtle vengeance." Her words were dry and dispassionate. "But you told Rasmussen."

"Yes. I had to. When Floyd assigned me the bank job last winter, I told him why I couldn't do it.

"He was marvelous about it! He patted me on the back for my integrity, and went away. I thought it was all okay, and he'd get somebody else to write the code, but he came back the next day and said he had no one else who could handle the project and the department couldn't afford to lose the contract. And he said that the fact I told him I'd done the other half proved more than anything else could that I could be trusted with the responsibility. He said the only real safeguard in life was personal integrity. North Bay trusted FSS and FSS trusted me.

"We used to joke about it, while I was blocking out the program, about the power I had over the little sidewalk tellers: how I could make them spit twenty-dollar bills all over Oakland at exactly twelve noon some Saturday.

"Now the federal insurance agency would rise or fall by my design. How a wrong branch would send bureaucrats out of tenth-floor windows.

"I felt like really hot stuff," she whispered. "It was a great couple months." Liz took the stuff of the drape in one hand. She leaned against the wall, head drooping.

"And I designed a really good piece of software. Nobody could have broken it. Except me."

One dark hand snaked out; Mayland Long turned on a lamp. In the soft yellow light Liz Macnamara looked lovely. The length of her arms and legs emphasized the slender fragility of her body. Her hair was like a sheet of glass, falling over her eyes. The taut, strained hands which wrung the fabric of the drape, however, were those of her mother, square and ordinary.

Long broke the silence. "Tell me about your father, Miss Macnamara."

She raised her head. Blinked. "Why? I haven't seen him in almost twenty years. It's not relevant to this."

His hands wove into their characteristic steeple pattern. "I reserve the right to ask irrelevant questions. Even impudent ones. You, of course, don't have to answer."

"My . . . my father is named Lars. Neil Lars. I refuse to use the name. He was a wind. Still is, probably, if he's still alive."

"Pardon? He's a what?"

Liz gestured vaguely. "A wind. He plays winds. Flute, mainly, but also piccolo, some oboe, clarinet. He ran off when I was a little kid. He's not involved in this."

"Are your parents divorced?" pressed Mr. Long stubbornly.

"Yes. Mother divorced him in absentia. Abandonment. He took all her money when he left. She used to say it was all 'gone with the wind.' "

He nodded. "That seems in character. Tell me more Miss Mac—Elizabeth. Was your father a tall man? Fair? Large boned?"

She nodded, mystified. "He was a huge, gorgeous Swede. He knew it, too."

"Why has your mother never remarried?" Long's eyes caught the light suddenly, gleaming like brass.

Liz shifted, foot to foot. "I don't know. Too busy, I guess. I'm glad she didn't. All the men she knew were losers, and her music is more important . . .

"Why do you ask?"

Long smiled at her confusion. "I want to know everything about your mother. It may help us locate her.

"But I interrupted a very interesting story. You wrote the second half of the security program and gave it to Rasmussen."

She nodded. "Then he asked to see a listing of what I had done for Carlo. Said he wanted to see what kind of criticism the old fool had made.

"I wasn't supposed to have one—a printout of the code—but I did. I kept it to spite Carlo. It was a mess: no structure, no comments. That's not my style, but I was being tricky when I wrote the thing, you see, because I knew I wasn't going to get credit for it. Carlo couldn't understand what was in it. No one could but me, I think. But he didn't have time to write it over, so he had to trust me that it worked."

"You are subtle," Long broke in. "And it was that incomprehensible listing you gave to Rasmussen?"

"Yes. I told him why I did it that way. He loved the joke. I thought. It was his idea to stick a wrench into the program to see if anyone would notice."

"What sort of wrench?"

Liz wandered over to the couch. She plucked up a tasseled pillow and hugged it to her. "I created a phoney account number which bled the bank of a thousand dollars a month. Rasmussen said we would just sit back and watch it get bigger and bigger until someone finally noticed. There was no theft involved, at this point. We didn't take the money. We just let it sit."

"And it was never noticed?"

Elizabeth raised her eyes from the pillow. "Doug Threve noticed. He worked for data processing at North Bay. He found the dummy account, but he's no engineer, couldn't get into the code to find out what was going on. He came to see Rasmussen, and I guess Floyd let the cat out of the bag."

"Did Threve . . . see the humor of the situation?"

Without warning the pillow went flying across the living room. It knocked an Escher print to the floor. "Did he? Hell! Goddamn, we were all such good friends! Threve, Rasmussen and Macnamara. Jolly bank robbers!"

She stood with her hands clenched uselessly in the air. Her hair covered her face like a veil.

Mayland Long cleared his throat.

"Herkneth, felowes, we thre been al ones, Lat ech of us holde up his hand til oother, And ech of us bicomen otheres brother."

These words recalled her from the tempest of her thoughts. "What did you say?"

"I quoted Chaucer. A bad habit, quotes."

"It sounded like Dutch." Elizabeth shuffled across the room to the fallen picture. There followed the plink of broken glass.

He measured her mood carefully before continuing.

"But I interrupted again. Another bad habit of mine. Am I to assume that it was Mr. Threve's idea that you three share the profits from this small bloodletting of North Bay Savings? He supplied credentials for the false account? Under whose name?"

"The name was Ima Heller." She spoke with distaste. "Rasmussen picked it—that's his kind of humor."

"That's the name on your mailbox," commented Long.

"Right. That's the name under which I bought this condo. Out of my account at North Bay. I've been Ms. Heller a lot, lately. Since the account is in a woman's name, we needed a woman to make all the personal appearances. And to take all the risks, of course, but I didn't realize that until later.

"Can you believe I went along with that?" Her words gritted. "A name like Ima Heller?" She stood cupping broken glass in her two hands.

Long regarded her from behind his hands. "How can I doubt you, when you speak with such sincerity?" He met her angry gaze and held it, smiling.

"Well, that was only the beginning. We emptied the account and went out on the town. Had a lot of fun. It wasn't serious then.

"I showed Threve what changes to make in the code to rake off more. We created phoney corporation accounts."

She approached the chair where he sat, swimming in shadow. The jagged glass in her hands sparkled as though she were holding diamonds. "In the past year we have pulled out of that bank two million dollars. I never decided to do it. I was still thinking whether it was right or it was wrong and I had done it. I can't even tell you why!"

"Elizabeth," said Mayland Long. "You've cut your hand on the glass."

7

Liz Macnamara thrust one hand beneath the running faucet. The water flowing down the drain was tinted pink. "The letter?" she echoed. "I did that when things began to go wrong, about a month ago."

"How did things begin to go wrong?" Mayland Long stood behind her in the kitchen. Absently he hefted the bottle he had left on the table. Golden liquid swirled about the sides. Elizabeth noticed.

"Oh! I'm sorry; I've forgotten all my manners. Can I get you a drink?"

"That's because I came in through the window. The formalities don't apply to visitors who come in through the window." A smile crept across his lean features: not a Chinese smile, but a very English smile, shy and diffident. "I believe I would like some of your excellent Scotch." The whiskey lapped and spattered within its confines of glass. "Isn't it lovely?" mused Long, "like bottled sunshine.

"And I do usually take it in a glass these days."

"Oh God, don't remind me. I might have killed you."

Long shook his head. "Not so easily as that."

She took the bottle from his hand, fetched another glass from the cupboard, and filled it for her guest. This homely task brought others to mind.

"What about food? It's dinner time. I've got some cold barbequed chicken in the fridge . . ." She opened the refrigerator door. "And French bread. And cake."

"You are very kind," sighed Mr. Long. He eased himself into a spindle-back kitchen chair and rubbed his face with both hands. His fingertips were hidden in his black hair. Then he sighed again and held the Scotch up to the light in contemplation.

"This matter of the letter at the bank," he reminded her. "When things began to go wrong . . ."

The plate she lay in front of him he recognized as Arabia china, from Finland. It was white as a northern winter, and at its edge ran a bold blue band. Long murmured to himself, "White plates and cups, clean gleaming, ringed with blue." The rest of the poem flashed unbidden through his mind, until he came upon the lines "the cool kindliness of sheets, that soon smooth away trouble; and the rough male kiss of blankets

. . . Sleep . . ." His eyes closed against the sight of red-stained chicken and the tawny length of bread crust.

Liz Macnamara stood attentive beside him, her own plate in her hand. "What did you say? After you asked me about the letter—was that Chaucer again?"

Long snapped awake. "Forgive me. No, it was Rupert Brooke, and I wasn't aware I was speaking aloud. I want to hear about the letter." He rubbed his fingers into his eye sockets, as though to punish his eyes for their treachery, and blinked a few times, focusing vaguely on the chocolate cake that sat on a doily in the middle of the table. Next to the cake lay an elegant, formidible knife with a rosewood handle and a blade five inches long.

Mayland Long was very much aware of the knife. He wondered that the young woman would trust him so much as to leave a weapon in his reach, when not a half hour ago she had been convinced he was an enemy. Did she leave it there as a test, having a gun concealed on her person? Did she assume fatalistically that if he were going to attack her he would have brought weapons of his own?

Long peered out of the corner of his eye at her as she sat down: tall, hard faced, ramrod straight. Was she the kind of cool gambler to whom the placement of a cake and a cake knife might be a move in a game of strategy?

When she had been duped by Peccolo, she had revenged herself quite creditably; the professor was still stinging from that, Long knew from personal experience. Yet within a year of that episode, she had allowed herself to be manipulated and badly used by Rasmussen. A smile twitched across Long's features. He saw Liz Macnamara as an eaglet, its first pinfeathers protruding through the coat of down. She was half pathetic, half dangerous, awkward and breakable at this stage in her life but promising power to come. That was, of course, if she survived.

And her survival had become Long's responsibility, somehow. He watched her and wondered what it would be like to be the father of a child.

She began to speak. "There's going to be an audit. Next week. Threve got scared. I don't know why; he'd been telling me all along that he could keep us bullet-proof.

"Anyway, instead of laying low, they started tapping the bank really heavily. No more individual withdrawals. It was all dipping into the corporation accounts. Hundreds of thousands of dollars at a time. And daily.

"I complained. I said they were making sure we couldn't survive the audit. And Rasmussen said then I ought to keep my mouth shut, because my part was done. Ima Heller wasn't necessary any more.

"And he said it wasn't any fun having a nagging broad around." She finished the sentence in steely composure. The chicken wing in her hand snapped in two. "Floyd's always been a walking pork roast!"

Immediately she shot a guilty look at Long. "I'm sorry. I didn't mean to offend you."

"Why would I be offended?" he replied. "I too have noticed the porcine element in Mr. Rasmussen's physiognamy. And character. On top of that he has an unpleasant laugh. Pray continue."

"Well, I wrote this letter and left it in my safe deposit box. Explaining all I've told you. I gave the key to Ellie Haig, of Surber and Haig. She's my lawyer. I call her every Monday, to check in. If I should miss a call she opens the box, where I left the letter in an envelope addressed to the police."

"I see. And you told Rasmussen about it."

"It was my trump card. I thought he couldn't touch me as long as I had that letter."

Long nodded. He tore a sheet from the roll of towels and fingered it absently. "It seems a sound idea. Why did you feel it necessary to call your mother?"

"I was frightened!" She shuddered. "As soon as I mentioned the letter, Threve got . . . ugly."

Neat black eyebrows shot up. "You could have simply left town."

"And wound up in prison, as soon as they audit the

bank. I'm the obvious suspect. I mean, as soon as the police squeezed Carlo, he would squeak. Then it would all be over for me. Not Doug or Floyd, just me.

"Oh, I should have gone to the police myself, I know. Confessed the whole thing," she said in a rush. "But I kept hoping I would find a way to make it right, first. I haven't spent that much of the money, you see—not like Floyd, who bought a yacht, or Doug with his Cessna and constant partying—and by working a few years I could make it up.

"I'm afraid of going to prison."

"You don't sound like a person who is afraid," remarked Long.

Stern blue eyes met his. "I know. I don't know how to show I'm afraid. Never have. I can be scared green about something—like now—and I come across as pissed off."

Liz scowled, tearing skin from the bone of the wing. "Sorry if my language bothers you. I can't think straight."

"No sort of language bothers me," he answered, "unless it's dull. But you looked quite frightened, Miss Macnamara, the first time I saw you."

"In the kitchen? Well you spooked the sh—you really startled me, there."

"No. I first saw you outside Rasmussen's office, about an hour ago. I followed you home."

She stared a moment. "What were you doing at RasTech?"

His answer came slowly, as finger by finger, he toweled the grease from his hands. "I was standing in the shrubbery, waiting for events. I expected the evening would produce Floyd Rasmussen. Instead, it has produced you. That was a change for the better, Elizabeth."

"Liz. And if I looked bad, the reason was that Floyd had just told me Threve had picked up my mother, and if I didn't go with him to the bank tomorrow morning . . ."

Liz paused and took a deep breath. Her hands

clenched together, blotched salmon and white. "They'd kill her."

Long's brown face remained impassive. He looked down at the remains of the meal. "Tomorrow morning," he said, and sighed. "I didn't know we had so little time.

"How did you think your mother's presence would neutralize a major felony, not to mention two major felons?" His words were mild—merely curious, and he did not look at Liz Macnamara as he spoke.

"If you knew my mother you wouldn't ask that question. But I didn't expect her to . . . neutralize the crime. I just wanted her to know all about it before I gave up and went to the police. I knew she'd stand by me. At first I was going to fly to New York and talk to her, but I had a hunch that my leaving town would put the wind up Floyd and Doug, and they'd be gone when I went to the police. That would have taken a lot of the impact out of a voluntary confession, you see. If it was found that my partners had already run out on me." The young woman shivered. "When I called Mother last week I didn't know what—monsters—those two were."

"Not monsters, Elizabeth," he murmured. "Merely thugs."

"Anyway, I decided that if I were going to dump the bad news on Mother, I'd treat her as well as I could in the process. It was kind of silly, really, because my mother doesn't care whether she sleeps on satin pillows or gunny sacks. Maybe I did it for my own sake, to salve my conscience, but I sent Mother two thousand dollars and told her to fly out first class. I made a week's reservation at the fanciest hotel I could find. In the City, I mean, not down here. I didn't want her *too* close to Floyd or Doug. I told her that I had to talk to her. I didn't tell her I was afraid."

"You didn't have to," said Mayland Long. The gentleness of his words caught her attention and she stared at him.

Food and drink had worked their magic on Mr. Long. His face flushed gold. His eyes glistened with lights of the same color. His left hand arced out in an involuted gesture, as though he followed threads in a tapestry only he could see. She followed his motion.

"Your mother can read signs in the air," he said. "The winds talk to her. She knew there was something very wrong with you and that is why she . . . let me help her find you." He let his gesture hang in the air. His eyes saw memories: a blue dress, a blue eye.

Liz Macnamara's eyes perceived an odd and unexpected beauty in the man's words and in the man. She blinked away the tears that terror alone had not brought forth.

He rose with boneless grace. His eyes were narrowed. He was thinking. Liz Macnamara stared up at him. "Where did she find you?"

"On a shelf," he answered, preoccupied. "I owe my involvement in your trouble to that gift you sent Marth—your mother."

She shook her head, not comprehending how a few thousand dollars could command the man before her. "Just get Mother away from those two and I'll work the rest of my life to pay you. I'll give anything. Do anything."

He became aware she was speaking. His gold eyes searched her face, puzzled, not following her words. A huge yawn caught him unaware. He shot a glare at the bottle, and he leaned one elbow on the refrigerator door.

"All I need," he said, "is a dark corner. And I only need it for a few hours."

"You need what? Why?"

He yawned again. "Because I'm tired. Too tired to think properly. It has taken a number of days to find you, Elizabeth, and I haven't slept much in that time.

"I have work to do tonight. It is a task important to our purpose, and best accomplished after nightfall. Between then and now . . ." He stepped forward, resting his hand on the back of her chair, "I must sleep. And since I haven't the time to drive to my rooms in San Francisco, I am asking you to put up with me."

"Of course." Liz Macnamara pushed herself away from the table. "But not in a corner. Please. Give me a minute to straighten up the bedroom." Dropping a rumpled paper towel into the wastebasket, she left the room.

He stared at the bed in horrified fascination. "I . . . I have heard of them, of course, but . . ."

Elizabeth dropped a hand to the undulating mattress, as though quieting a huge beast. "It's just a waterbed. It's really comfortable. Not cold at all." Seeing his expression unchanged, she half-smiled. "Don't be afraid." She left him, closing the door behind her.

He was dubious but also very weary. Mr. Long undressed, folded his clothes, and gave himself to the embrace of the waves.

Liz spent the next two hours seated at the kitchen table. Her mind raced wildly, without traction. At nine she cracked the bedroom door to wake Mr. Long. The vertical thread of light happened to fall over the form on the sheets. He was bronze, like a statue, and his skin appeared as tight to the body and as hard as the finish of a bronze statue. He lay sprawled with the dramatic indifference of a statue, also. One arm was tossed up in line with the lean torso, and the back-tilted head repeated the angle. The other arm, the left arm, was flung outward, and the fingers grasped air. There was passion in the pose: passion and a quality of abandonment quite foreign to the presence who had shared her meager dinner.

And it was this attitude, more than the fact that the sleeper had thrown off the sheet and lay naked in the light, which impelled Liz Macnamara to close the door again and knock.

"Thank you," Mr. Long said, stepping out of the door fully clothed. "I'm surprised. I didn't really expect to fall asleep on that contrivance."

He glanced behind him at the digital clock, which shone its red numbers silently beside the bed. He felt in his pocket for keys. "Please do me one more favor. I need addresses for both Rasmussen and Threve."

Her first attempt at a reply choked her. "Do you need to see them? Tonight?"

"I do. But it is not necessary for either of the gentlemen to see me. I want someone to lead me to your mother, Miss Macnamara. It has to be tonight."

She took a step forwards. "I'll come too."

Long frowned. "It has taken me three days to find you, Elizabeth. If I lose you again . . ."

"You won't. I want to go with you. I can't take sitting here alone." She was two inches taller than Long. Her frosty eyes bore a challenge. "Why should you go out and I stay here?"

"I think it likely Rasmussen or Threve will call to check up on you tonight. If you are not home they may think you have abandoned your mother and run off. Or they may believe you are out to work them mischief, as indeed you would be. Either way I think they will react by killing their hostage."

Liz's teeth ground together, but she made no answer. Instead she blundered about in a desk drawer for paper and pencil.

As she wrote she was speaking. "There. Rasmussen lives in Santa Clara. Big house: he used to be married. Threve has an apartment. I drew maps."

He took the paper and looked at it for twenty seconds. Then he put it down. "Burn this," he dictated. "And close your address book. Under no circumstances must your colleagues find out you've seen me."

Liz Macnamara was staring at Long's shirt. Her eyes held sudden doubt. "You're going burgling like that?"

His left eyebrow rose. "What exactly do you mean, Elizabeth, 'like that?' "

"That shirt almost glows in the dark."

Inspiration hit Liz Macnamara. Inspiration and the memory of a very thin dark body on the bed. "Wait here," she commanded. "Don't go away."

She returned in two minutes, to find Mr. Long sitting

obediently where she had left him. Instead of jeans she was wearing a mint green satin dressing gown. Green was a color that suited her very well.

She carried a bundle. "Here," she announced. "These are . . . more appropriate, I think. The sweatshirt is gray, and blue jeans don't stand out in the dark."

He rose and said "No." He said it with great authority.

"Yes. It's my mother," she replied.

His face was unyielding.

"What if you have to climb a fence? What if you have to run? If Threve or Rasmussen catch up with you and shoot you, or hit you on the head or something—well that's a pretty high price for both of us to pay for your vanity."

"Vanity?" echoed Long. His eyes flashed yellow.

"Vanity," she insisted, as the clothes slipped from her arms and tumbled to the floor. "Please. For my mother's sake."

Mayland Long folded before the urgency in her voice. "You are so much like your mother," he sighed, stooping to retrieve the outfit. "And I . . . I am not at all what I was at the beginning of the week.

"They will not fit," he predicted, as he vanished again into the bedroom.

"They *do* fit," she crowed in triumph.

"I admit it," replied Long. He was a very different seeming man, in faded jeans and a sweatshirt.

He did not look so old, since age generally follows on tailoring. He did not look so terribly well bred, since class follows the same rules. Most obviously, he did not look half as self-satisfied as he had before.

His left hand pulled at his right sleeve, which was too short for his arms.

"I think you look fine!" she stated, surveying all she had done to Mr. Long. "And now there's nothing white about you.

"Oh! I'm sorry."

He laughed. His teeth denied her words. "What

would you have done had I had the coloring of Mr. Rasmussen?

"Or your own fairness," he added, his gaze halted on the young woman's face.

"Shoe polish," she replied, smiling for the first time since he had met her.

He transferred his wallet to his jeans pocket. "Ah! While I remember, Elizabeth."

"Liz."

"Liz. Yes. You are supposed to surrender that letter tomorrow. Don't. Create a copy and give Rasmussen that."

"That can't work. I thought of it already. Rasmussen knows I wrote the letter on an 8080 text processor at RasTech. I can't get back to copy it without being seen."

He was stopped by this, and stood motionless for half a minute. "Then I have to return by dawn tomorrow. If I haven't found your mother yet, I'll have a copy of that letter for you to surrender."

"How will you do that?"

"I'll print one," he replied confidently.

"You . . . know how to use the system?"

His gesture was reassuring. "That's no problem. But if dawn comes and I fail to show . . ."

"No!" she cried out. Then she spoke more reasonably. "What do I do if you fail to show?"

"Go to the police."

"But they'll kill her! Threve said if the police showed up anywhere around . . ." She put her hand to her mouth and bit down, so that she would not start shaking again.

Mayland Long stepped closer. One hand against her yellow hair pulled her head gently to his shoulder. He could feel her body tremble. Slowly and clearly he whispered in her ear. "Elizabeth, these men intend to kill your mother. Only if there is no one left alive who knows, can they escape suspicion."

The trembling died away. She mumbled something that was lost into the fabric of Long's shirt.

"I didn't hear that," he whispered, suddenly conscious of her hair against his face and her warm, moist breath on his neck.

Liz Macnamara took one step back and stood alone. "I said I know. They intend to kill mother as soon as they can kill me. And they'll do that as soon as they have the letter. I'm not even sure she's alive now. I asked to hear her voice and Floyd said later."

"She's alive," said Long. "I'm sure of it."

She didn't ask him to explain his certainty. "But what shall I do till you come back? To help, I mean."

He smiled. "Sleep, if you can. If not, then drink Scotch. Or pray. Survive in your own way; I can't know what's best for you, Elizabeth.

"Til morning," he concluded, bowing slightly. He flicked off the light and pulled wide the courtyard window. Cold mist from the fountain blew in with the breeze. There was no sound from the gulls asleep in the grass.

8

Martha Macnamara awoke with a miserable aching nose. It felt as though it had been stuffed for two weeks straight. Her hands were cramped; she must have been lying on them. There was something else bothering her as well; it took her a few confused minutes to figure out what that was.

"Oh!" she cried out. "I have to go to the bathroom." She opened her eyes, and the results were so unpleasant she closed them again. The ceiling had looked so ugly, and it swept by with unsettling speed. The spinning ceiling was mere dizziness, of course, like the time she had had her wisdom teeth pulled. And the ugliness must be a result of nausea; dizziness and nausea always went together.

But why was she nauseated? Why dizzy? And why couldn't she place that ceiling she had glimpsed, with its acoustic tile and round fluorescent lights?

Where was she? Where should she be?

Not at home; her own ceiling was plastered, with a crack through it like a lightning bolt, and the fixtures wore white paper lanterns. Besides, Martha knew she was not at home; she was staying at the James Herald Hotel. Which did not look anything like this. Those ceilings were arched, and the picture moldings were impressively Corinthean.

She felt so awful that maybe she was in a hospital. Yes. She had passed out on the street. Someone in a black car had spoken her name . . .

And now she just had to go to the bathroom, dizzy or not. She pulled her eyes open.

How very odd. She was stretched out flat on a table. Brightly colored lengths of wire were wrapped around her wrists, tying them together in front of her.

"Out that door and to the left," said a voice. She searched for the speaker.

He sat sprawled in a white director's chair, amidst a clutter of magazines. He was a small man whose dark hair was carefully slicked back and curled about the ears. He wore a wine-red shirt which hung open, revealing a gold medallion. His belt was wide and black, his trousers white. His voice matched his appearance perfectly.

Martha tried to sit up; it was a hopeless effort.

"I can't do anything without my hands."

He stared insolently and flung another magazine to the floor. He lounged across the barren room toward her. In his hands were black steel dikes. he snipped through the skinny windings on her wrists.

"Try to run and I'll break your leg," he said, as she slipped off the wooden table. "There's nowhere to go, anyway."

He was quite correct. The tall, barnlike room had no windows and only two doors. One of the two was green metal. It had a key lock and a hole beneath where the doorknob had once been. The other door stood open, and as Martha passed through it, leaning on the doorsill for support in her vertigo, she saw that it led through a short hall to two other doors. One of them was identical to the door in the large room, except that it had a knob on it. The other door was wood.

She turned the knob on the green door. It was locked. "Other door," came the voice behind her. It was a nasty voice, the sort of voice which might make a child cry, hearing it say "other door" in that sneering fashion. It was the sort of voice that would want to. Martha turned and passed through the wooden door.

"You are very mistaken in this," repeated Martha. "No one I know has more than four hundred dollars in the bank."

"The less I hafta say, the better off you'll be," grumbled her captor, as he rummaged around on the floor. He had leafed through all his magazines while his prisoner was unconscious, not reading them, but reading the captions on all the pictures and spoiling the interest of them, and so now had nothing to read.

"You've said that twice in the last hour, and you must know by now it doesn't shut me up."

He raised his eyes. "Less you say, happier I'll be," he added.

Mrs. Macnamara sat only a few feet from his chair. A small pile of discarded magazines kept her from the chill of the floor. Her feet were folded on her thighs in the full lotus posture. She had spent a large part of the day in this position, and now daylight was fading from the crack beneath the green door. Had it been just one day since the trip to the Valley and the lunch in the tea shop with Mayland Long?

She remembered the car, and how a man had leaned out, smiling, and taken her hand. She remembered the open door. The yank on her arm. The hankie with its operating-room stink.

That was how she got her nose burned, she decided. Ether, or chloroform, or whatever.

Had no one seen this? Where was Mayland? He'd been right beside her. He just found that flower, and given it to her. So very romantic, but silly, too, in his dignified, almost pedantic manner. Had they snatched him too? Had they killed him? The thought was unbearable.

And what about Liz? A spasm of fear nearly cut off Mrs. Macnamara's breathing. Liz was the hub around which all this mystery revolved. Though Martha Macnamara pleaded ignorance of the affair, pretending to assume she was being held for ransom, she knew that her capture was tied in with her daughter's trouble. Oh Liz, Liz! What had she done to herself?

And what a silly grief it would be to her to find that her mother was kidnapped, just because she had called her for help. Or that her mother was dead.

The floor glinted with brass snippets. Huge soft dust kitties rolled ponderously whenever the man threw a magazine.

Except for the table on which Martha had awakened, a dirty white refrigerator, and the director's chair—also white, also dirty—the room was empty. No sound leaked in from the outside world.

Martha felt despair well up from her chest to her throat. She let it sit there, paying attention to her breathing instead.

The first drops of rain spattered against the windshield. Long had been expecting them since the wind turned from the north. The wet air summoned a host of visions to his mind—the bare, black cliffs in the rocks above Taipei. Old eyes filmed with blue, and a mouth of bad teeth, rudely laughing. Laughing at him, while the rain came down. He shook his head against these inchoate memories.

The freeway was quiet, at 9:45 on this Thursday evening, but it was treacherous with the first rain of the season. He kept the speedometer hovering around seventy-five. The neon signs of bars and cheap motels sparkled by, diffracted in each clinging drop.

He believed that Martha was not dead. He believed this strongly, but it gave him no feeling of security, because it was a belief not under his control. If suddenly that belief went out, like a candle—a candle in the rain . . .

He hit a pothole, skidded across the lane and recovered automatically. His conviction that Martha was alive was not a feeling like his anger, which he could test and find durable. It was rather a gift from outside, and Long had never trusted gifts.

Pink billows of oleander filled the median strip. Long's thoughts drifted to Liz Macnamara. He relived his interview with her: her courage and her terror, her sudden shifts of mood, the remarkable concessions he had found himself making to her.

She was like her mother, yes, but much stormier. And at the same time, more fragile. He remembered her head on his shoulder, her hair against his face. He was disturbed, not by the incident, but by his reaction to it.

But mankind had always been like that, turned off its course by a step, by the turn of a mouth, by a covert glance, or scented hair. Should he be any different? His teeth ground together as he considered; was he any different? He was alone with the hiss of wet tires on wet concrete.

He turned off both engine and lights on Dover Park Avenue, and he coasted to a stop by the curb.

The world was gray and insular, filled with rain. His excellent hearing listened for more. He heard televisions. The thin voice of public entertainment floated from house after house as he walked. The same two speakers, repeated endlessly. No conversation. No music.

Rain beaded on his heavy black hair and in his

eyelashes. It was not so bad to be wet, while the weather was warm.

Rasmussen's neighborhood was new; it lacked street-lights. Mr. Long passed down the street invisibly, the sound of his footsteps swallowed by the rain.

The house took shape from the grayness. It sprawled on a low hill, set on a corner a little apart from its neighbors. A board set on a spike by the street announced the address.

The sloping yard had been sodded quite recently. The scars between the strips had not healed; they bled red clay. No garden, outcrop nor tree interfered with the sweep of lawn to the house. The doorway was flat against the wall of the house, and that wall itself was white stucco. The windows were dim, but somewhere within the shell of the house at least one light was lit. Gazing along the prospect of the sidewalk, his sigh melted into that of the rain.

The back of the house was much like the front, except that from there the light was brighter.

Mayland Long squatted down, resting his palms on the glistening sidewalk. For thirty seconds he tested the silence. Then he stepped onto the grass.

The thick plush of root and blade was reassuring, almost intoxicating to his hands as he half-crawled up the slope toward the house. Fearing his silhouette against the bright wall he lowered himself flat upon the grass and began a slow circuit of the house.

The wall he had approached was broken by five windows. The middle one was frosted glass: obviously the bathroom. Three of the others were tall framed and clear. Bedrooms? The one at the rear of the house emitted a faint yellow glow. It was wider than the rest. He guessed it to be the kitchen.

This wall faced a side street, and beyond, a low growth of scrub which had stolen back land the builders had ravaged and left. He stood, peering through the rain-runneled glass of the rightmost window.

It was a bedroom, but unused by the look of it. The

mattress on its Harvard frame lay gleaming in the night.
A small bureau stood against the far wall. No mirror.
Once it had been a boy's room, perhaps.

The window frame was new, and bore a bolt lock. He
looked beyond the window and through the room, to
where a door stood open, revealing a hall with staircase.
Across the hall from the bedroom door was the living
room. He caught his breath with a small, satisfied sound.
On the far side of the parlor, against the opposite wall of
the house, stood a pair of french doors.

He dropped once more to the ground and began to
crawl toward these.

Beneath the kitchen window he paused to listen.
There was no television to be heard. No movement at
all. A cat murred once, perhaps next door.

When he came to the patio which opened out from the
french doors he took off his shoes, and wiped the mud
from his hands onto the grass. Neither the knees of his
jeans nor the front of his sweatshirt had gotten muddy.

He stood at last, examining the parlor from around the
edges of bright print curtains. The furniture was all a set:
of pine, heavy and crude. Some pieces of it still wore
strips of bark. The head of a deer hung on the left hand
wall, its idiot gaze fixed on the stones of the fireplace.
Beneath it stood a spindle-sided magazine rack, empty.

The door was locked with a bolt like that on the
bedroom window. But the door was made of small panes
of glass held in place by wooden mullions. With his
fingertips he peeled one of these strips away, and then
another. After the third minton was removed, a rectangle of glass slipped into his hand. He reached in and slid
back the bolt.

He stood dripping in the silent room. It was warm in
the house, and as he ran his hand through his head,
releasing a spatter of drops, he realized that his few
hours sleep had not sufficed. He was still weary.

And he had so much to do. Since it seemed Rasmussen was not receiving this evening, he had to gain what
information he could from the house itself. He needed to

find the address of the place where Martha was being held. He needed to find it tonight, before Threve and Rasmussen got their hands on what they thought was Liz's letter, and both women's lives became superfluous to their plans.

If he could not find the information here, then he must go to Threve's apartment and try again. But that would require time and risk. He felt pressured on both counts.

He began with the room he was in, working with quick eyes in the dimness. The barbaric furniture held few drawers or hiding places. The mantel was bare. Rasmussen's house seemed much neater than his office. Perhaps the man had a housekeeper.

A sharp hiss announced that he was not alone in the room. He swiveled from the waist, very fast, to confront the outrage of a startled white cat, which stood frozen on the stairs, tail stiff and bristling. It snarled at the intruder and lifted one snowy forepaw, displaying its armament.

For an instant cat and man faced one another, the lean rigidity in the posture of the one reflected in that of the other. Then the man relaxed. He sank down on one knee and averted his eyes. A throaty trilling filled the room: a soft, comfortable cat-sound.

The thrashing of the cat's tail subsided. Pink-rimmed ears unfolded. The white cat stalked closer.

Long centered his small noise deeper in his throat. It became a purr. It ceased. As the cat reached him, he extended his hand—felt it butted by the blunt, white skull.

"I have no argument with you, little warrior," he whispered, as brown eyes lost themselves in green.

At that moment the room was blasted with light. The white cat leaped straight into the air as Mayland Long spun about and froze, staring straight down the barrel of a twenty-two rifle. It might have been the cat that hissed.

Martha wanted to ask the fellow about Mr. Long, but it was possible the kidnapper hadn't noticed Long, and any mention of her companion might imperil him. Liz, she assumed, was already neck-deep in this.

The man in the red shirt was peering into the ancient refrigerator that stood against one wall. Martha noticed he had a dust mark on the seat of his white trousers shaped like an upside-down heart. There was a rattle of beer cans.

She realized she was very thirsty. "Can I have a beer?" she asked.

"No," he said, surly. He didn't look at her.

This small nastiness roused her. "Why the hell not? You've got a whole six pack."

"They're mine. I don't want to waste them."

Hearing these words, Martha felt a cold certainty that the little man intended to kill her.

She was afraid of dying. She believed anyone who claimed not to be was either a liar or had never been close to death. But her fear was of manageable size; she could endure it.

If Liz were to die, however, at the age of twenty-four, bright and strong, having known so much hardship and so little fun in her short life . . . Martha knew that she herself was being kept prisoner as bait in some sort of trap for her daughter. She refused to be so used. She would die first. Or kill.

Settling again into the lotus pose, her bound hands resting on her lap, she stared about her at the dirty, depressing room, empty as a dry skull. The little kidnapper returned to his chair, a bottle sweating in his hand. He belched loudly.

It was hard to believe that just yesterday (or was it now the day before?) she had sat across the table from Mayland Long, the two of them pretending that the world was essentially civilized and had been created for the sake of play. Theirs had been expensive play, too. She recalled the dazzling chandeliers of the James Herald Hotel. She recalled Mayland Long's strange, mutable eyes.

Better to die tonight, having known him, than to have

died alone last week in New York, in the August stink and heat.

And even if she died tonight. Even if *he* were already dead . . . the fact that he had lived and been who he was: elegant, diffident, kindly, with his funny hands and gorgeous rich voice. That meant something. That they had met meant something, too: dying now could not erase that.

Martha's thoughts sank to the bottom of her mind, leaving it attentive and quiet. The kidnapper stared at her with distrust upon his features. Her stillness frightened him.

9

"Why, it's Mr. Long," boomed Rasmussen, smiling hugely. "What a surprise! And looking like something the cat dragged in."

He received no answer. "Couldn't you guess I'd have an alarm system rigged up in this house?"

Long was a moment in replying. "I didn't take that into consideration, Mr. Rasmussen. I confess I've underestimated you." Wet, ill-dressed and preternaturally calm, he regarded the threatening gun.

"May I stand up?"

The big blond stared over the scope sight. At a range of ten feet, the sight was more of a hindrance than a help.

"Why not?" He moved back a few steps, to prevent Long from slipping in beside the gunbarrel. "And then you can tell me what you're doing in my house. Besides breaking the law, of course."

Mr. Long climbed to his feet. His movements reflected the stiffness of age. "We both know very well," he began, "that I am looking for Elizabeth Macnamara."

"I told you yesterday I don't know where she is." Rasmussen's voice sharpened.

Long's remained quiet. "Obviously I did not believe you yesterday."

The rifle moved a bit, as Rasmussen perfected his aim. Through an effort of will, Long kept his eyes not on the trigger, but on Rasmussen's ruddy face.

"Obviously." Rasmussen was silent for a moment as he considered the situation. Then the mask of amiability disappeared from his face. Long saw and understood.

"Whatever pay you got, buddy, it wasn't enough," muttered the blond.

"Did you call the police when the alarm sounded?" Long stalled, shifting his weight to one foot. "Or do you plan to present them with a fait accompli: the corpus of one aging burglar."

The muzzle of the gun followed his movement efficiently. "I haven't called yet," mumbled Rasmussen. "Maybe I will later. I haven't decided what's the cleanest way out of this."

Rasmussen found his grin again and put it on. "You know, fella, you're totally in the wrong, being found in my living room like this. In the legal sense, I mean."

Mayland Long lifted his eyebrows; his eyes were opaque. "The legal sense? Would you care to discuss others?"

The smile stuck to Rasmussen's face, quite irrelevant. "You put me in this position," he growled, his full cheek against the black metal of the rifle. "And now I have to do this. I really hate it."

He breathed in slowly, then let half the breath out and pulled the trigger.

The rifle coughed, but Long was not standing before it. Rasmussen's exhalation had been as much of a signal as the dark man needed. He moved with the abruptness of a startled lizard, sideways, sailing three feet above the carpet, and he vanished up the stairs.

Rasmussen cursed and followed. On the landing he hesitated, peering into the unlit reaches above. His left hand fumbled in his trouser pocket with a clip of twenty-two shorts.

The second floor of the house was a single large chamber, originally an attic. At each gable end were semicircular windows of leaded glass. The only other openings were skylights, set high in the roof. In the center of the floor stood a velvet couch and loveseat. Against the wall was a heavy liquor bar of oak and brass. Beneath the far wall, under a window gleaming red and gold, sat an enormous pedestal bed. A corner of the room to the right of it had been enclosed to create the bathroom.

Long took this all in as he leaped out from the stairwell. The bathroom was a trap: no way out. The bar might conceal him, but its confinement would also hold him helpless. The carpet was white plush. With the lights on, Mr. Long would stand out like a sparrow in the snow.

The lack of windows was the worst part of it; there was no escape from this place. He heard Rasmussen's feet upon the stairs.

There was a small door set into the left-hand wall. It was less than four feet high and very narrow. He darted toward it, pausing only to plunge his fingers into the dryboard of the wall and yank out the light switch.

In the still darkness behind the wall he picked his way. This triangular space had no flooring; support beams alternated with soft, treacherous strips of insulation. He sank again to hands and feet and crawled away from the entrance.

The passage ended above the stairwell. It turned no corners. There was no exit. He turned around and waited.

Rasmussen's progress was unmistakable; Long could hear the weight of his passing in the creak of the support beams. He stood above the stairs, put his hand to the wall and cursed aloud. The rifle shifted against the man's shoulder, Rasmussen, too, began to wait.

Mr. Long was no claustrophobe. This musty hole comforted him, and he weighed his alternatives.

Up until now his choices had been forced. He had headed for the stairs because they were dark. Had the rifleman been fool enough to stand closer to his intended victim, Long would have gone for his attacker. As it was, he had had to slink into this blind hole, lacking other concealment.

But his enemy was at a small disadvantage, now, with no light available except that of the drizzling heavens. If he attempted to pursue Long behind the wall, this disadvantage would become severe. If Rasmussen stumbled into the darkness, the game would belong to Long.

The biggest danger was that the man might find some sort of light. But it was doubtful he kept a flash in the master bedroom, and if he went downstairs to fetch one, that would give Long valuable time.

Time not to escape this house but to change the balance of power.

Old instincts awoke in Long's memory: old and no longer quite familiar. He knew what it was to hunt. He also remembered, though less well, what it was to be hunted. His lips shrank back from his teeth.

Rasmussen put his back to the wall. He was very close. Long, hearing the scrape of his shirt, considered breaking through the flimsy wall and taking Rasmussen by the throat. He decided against this because it was more important to question the rifleman than to kill him.

Rasmussen edged by. Eight feet from the small door he stopped. The muted smack of a twenty-two cartridge cut the silence. Another. Rasmussen was methodically piercing the shadows with bullets.

One shell buried itself in the wall behind the bar. One cracked tile. One glanced off metal and sang down the stairway.

And then five bullets in quick succession slammed through the flimsy panels of the little door. The smell of powder cut into the air. Rasmussen inserted a new clip. The door was jerked open.

Standing just outside, Rasmussen shot diagonally into the corridor, first left, then right. Long dared not move.

Then the gunman stepped off the floor, giving his weight hesitantly to a beam.

A shot into the wall behind Long sent a shower of powder around his head. Rasmussen raised the barrel of the gun above his head and brought it down on the other side of the narrow passage. He fired and turned again.

Long moved toward him. His face was only inches above the insulation, fine as angel hair.

This methodical attack was original and deadly. Long had depended on fear of discovery to make his opponent stingy with his fire. But the spit of this rifle was hardly louder than the pre-recorded violence emitted from the tv's along the street. It would be lost in the rain.

If this continued, he would inevitably be hit.

But there was a weakness in Rasmussen's strategy; he had to divide his time between the left and right passage. During those moments Long crawled toward Rasmussen.

The air sparked by his left ear. The noise of the shot was deafening. Then Rasmussen turned and he was free to move. The rifle swung back and Long froze again.

Twice more and he would be able to touch Rasmussen.

The bullet hit Long in the right shoulder and smashed his collarbone. Passing through flesh it buried itself in the wooden frame post beside him. White teeth flashed in dumb shock.

He felt his right hand slide from its grip on wood. It caught against splinters as it fell, and came to rest finally in the bed of insulation. The arm was useless; it had been taken from him and replaced with a focus of astounding pain.

Instinct alone kept Long quiet. He shifted his weight to the left and brought his right leg forward. He had no choice but to attack now, before Rasmussen had time to turn and fire again: little hope, but no choice. Long lifted himself from the beam and stood swaying. Measuring the distance, he crouched to spring.

But Rasmussen stood motionless, his rifle pointed at the ceiling. His head was tilted, listening.

Long heard the noise too. It came from outside the passage—from the bathroom. He identified the sound with no trouble.

Rasmussen turned, nearly losing his footing. He bulled his way through the narrow door. Long recognized this as his moment.

He recognized it, and yet he did not attack. He tapped his bottled anger, commanding it to flare up, heat his nerves, impel him with the certainty of violence—the single-souled violence of a wounded beast which fuels ferocity with pain.

There was no response from within. Merely the recognition. And the pain.

It might have been the ignominy of his condition— wet, ill from lack of sleep, dressed like a sidewalk tramp and barefoot—which blocked his response. It might have been the blood which even now filtered through the gauzy fiberglass and spread a sad pink stain through the plaster of the child's empty bedroom below. It might have been that civilization had penetrated too deeply into him.

It might have been that he was old.

Long slunk out from the passage behind Rasmussen and faded down the staircase. He heard three shots, and a high-pitched yowl cut off. He heard Rasmussen's cry of frustration and rage. He opened the french door quietly and stooped for his shoes, clenching his teeth around a groan.

He had known it was the cat.

The rain had slowed. A few stars burnt through the cloud. Mayland Long wove into the scrub wood across from Rasmussen's house. He put his back to a tree and waited for Rasmussen to come out.

For nothing had been changed by this little *pas de deux*. Long still had to find Martha Macnamara. Rasmussen must lead him to her. With his quarry escaped, the man would have to move.

Liz was still safe, since Rasmussen didn't know Long had found her. She would remain safe until the banks opened tomorrow. Martha must be alive. He could say no more.

Chill seeped out of the earth and air. It invaded his anatomy. Blood and water mixed beneath the tree where he sat.

Why had he failed himself? He felt he had reacted in a manner alien to his own nature, and he was very familiar with his nature; it had been with him a long time. He ought to have taken Rasmussen as soon as the man's back was turned. Had he killed the man it would have been unfortunate, but understandable. That was proper behavior, with logic and the fire of the beast in harmony. Instead he had run away.

Tentatively, he sorted his feelings. Was he ready to confront Rasmussen again, if need be?

Where was his anger?

He was rewarded for his probing with cold, deadly pain. His vision swam with meaningless stars. His ears filled with a pounding, like surf. Mayland Long passed out under the weeping trees.

Martha had not noticed the box before. It lay hidden amid a pile of trash the small man had accumulated during the day: candy wrappers, soda cans, broken cigarettes. He pulled it out now, brushing the ash from the black plastic grill on the top of it.

She stared grimly at the cassette recorder. She knew what it was for and she had guessed events would come to this.

A magazine jacket covered with print caught her desperate eye. "*Dr. Dobb's!*" she chirped. "I know someone else who reads that."

His eyes held only boredom and contempt. His fingers fiddled with the machine. He drew the microphone out of its compartment and plugged it in the back of the box.

"Now, lady. It's time for you to talk to your daughter."

She regarded him with birdlike intensity, her blue eyes unblinking. His own face flushed, heavy and sullen.

"Just tell her you're all right. Tell her to do what we say." He pressed the record and play buttons.

The whirr of the moving tape was the only sound in the room. Martha Macnamara's small mouth was pursed. With her round face and tangled braids she was the image of rebellion.

He stopped the tape. Smacked her backhanded across the face. Rewound and started again.

"Talk," he grunted. She stared at nothing, across the room.

The man hit Martha three more times. The last time he hit her, he used his fist. "Talk!" he bellowed. His voice cracked. The tape reached its end and the machine snapped off.

Martha Macnamara abruptly began talking. "You spend a lot of money on your clothes," she observed, through cracked lips. "But you don't know how to put them together. With white trousers you should not wear a bright red shirt. Except in Italy, maybe . . ."

His finger jabbed the rewind. He stood looking down at his captive, grinding his teeth. He kicked her. Kicked her again, just below the wire-bound hands.

"Ow, owww, owww!" shrieked Martha Macnamara. "Yow Owww!" She cried out once for every kick, loudly and with great animation. He pressed record once more, and the tape filled with wordless howls and yelps.

The small man turned away, purple faced. He leaned against the wall, slicking back his hair, and stood in unconscious parody of Michelangelo's *David*. He did not see Martha stagger to her feet, pluck up the recorder by the mike cord, swing it around her head, and send it crashing against the back of his neck.

He tottered and fell, but as the machine was made of light plastic, he did not lose consciousness. As Martha bent over him, scrabbling through his pockets for the keys and dikes, his arms shot up and grabbed her by the throat.

"*I'll kill you, you bitch!*" he roared. The woman's head snapped back and forth as he shook her and squeezed. Her face was mottled, under the bruises.

The green door suddenly opened and the small man looked up into small eyes set in a huge head, a head gold and spiky as an Aztec platter.

"Jesus Christ, Threve, what'd you *do* that for?" gritted Floyd Rasmussen.

10

Mayland Long woke under a cold clear sky. With an agony of effort he pulled himself to his feet. A cautious walk down the sidewalk in front of Rasmussen's house told him the man had made his escape, for the lights were all out and the french door closed once again. Around the square where Long had removed the glass the injured wood gleamed white.

He didn't curse himself for his body's latest failing; he merely proceeded down the street toward his car, each step premeditated, slowly . . .

Long felt about as sick as a man can be, still standing. Wet cold ate into his lungs; his breath steamed. He cradled his right arm in front of him. A dull pounding in his ears had haunted him through dreams into miserable wakefulness. Its dull thunder confused him, though he knew it was his own heartbeat.

Worse than the cold, worse than the confusion, almost worse than the lancing pain in his shoulder was the thirst. If he could find water, he could bear the cold and the pain.

Oily puddles in the road tempted him. Had they been deeper he might have bent to drink from them. If he were able to bend. The car. Was there water anywhere in it? Perhaps in the washer reservoir.

But no. That water would be mixed with antifreeze. Thoughtfully he regarded the dark houses he passed. Water in the garden faucets? In the green plastic hoses coiled in the grass? His steps slowed—stopped.

He didn't dare. If he were caught, found by some insomniac householder, staggering bloodsoaked and frozen among the dahlias, or if there were a dog . . . He could go without water. For a little while.

The Citroën gleamed under starlight. He found his keys, but his hand was not steady and he had difficulty unlocking the door. He pulled it open and sank into the tan leather seat. Wherever he touched it, the leather darkened: brown with water, russet with blood.

In the comfort of the car he rested, until faintness rose up from his chest to his throat and threatened to drown him. Words echoed in his head. Tinny, removed, without meaning . . . "In order to become what you are not, it is necessary to go by a way in which you are not."

Whose words? Who had said that? Long's distracted mind pursued the question. Donne? No. Not like Donne. They were from a poem of Eliot's. Or . . . were they the Formosan's? The old man in the rain. Rain again . . . Whatever, they made no sense. Didn't help at all. Never had. Words.

What would help? He needed . . . rest. There were so many miseries, crowding him close. Pain, thirst, cold, worry, loss. It hurt to think. It hurt to breathe.

Failure.

Suddenly it occurred to Mayland Long that he didn't know what to do next. He couldn't remember. Staring into the darkness, broken only by the pale arc of the steering wheel before him, he shuddered.

It was rest he needed, he told himself. He would

regain both memory and strength if he could rest. Where to look for it?

Long could not recall his childhood, nor any time he was under the care of others. He had not been ill in many years. He conjured up a vision of his sitting room like an animal yearning for its den, yet there was nothing within those book-lined walls that had the power to comfort him now. Nothing called to him but sleep.

Blankness soared toward him on owl's wings.

His eyes opened and his head jerked up. He remembered his commitments. Both to Martha Macnamara and to Elizabeth, he had made promises. Because he was born in China, he had a great respect for promises. Because he had always kept them, Long believed most strongly in his own promises, and knew that a promise he did not fulfill would fulfill itself upon him. Live or dead, no creature might escape the unfolding of its own actions.

He turned on the engine.

And the heat.

Elizabeth's bedroom was green. The bedside lamp gave off a gauzy light, like filtered sunlight falling on the forest floor. The lamp, the table beneath it, the dresser, the standing cheval mirror—all were of golden oak. The bedroom was just the way she wanted it. It was one of the few things in her life that were just the way she wanted.

She sought solace in that room, beneath the rumpled covers of the great waterbed. As she had assured Mr. Long, the bed was quite warm. Within her was the additional golden warmth of Scotch. She hugged her down pillow.

Her mind revolved endlessly on one question. How had she gotten involved in this horror? The question had become a ritual exercise, for she already knew the answer: it was a union of philosophy and greed.

What made transfer of property sometimes morally justifiable and sometimes theft? Mutuality was a good criterion. When one took and gave nothing, that was theft. But the bank might take one's car away, when one was down on one's luck and needed the car most. That was lawful behavior on the bank's part, but was it morally justifiable? And if transfer of property could be justified, was it the idea of transfer, or of property itself which sat at the root of the problem?

Pragmatism was a sword that cut through such knots; an action was to be judged by its consequences alone. Liz had been introduced to the philosophy as a penniless freshman in college and had lived by it. There was nothing wrong in a deed which hurt no one and did the doer much good.

Liz's sophisticated robbery was of that kind. No one was hurt but the federal insurance agency, and Liz's own situation was marvelously improved. Of course, if everyone followed her lead, the bank would break and individuals would be hurt, but everyone was not robbing the bank. Only Liz Macnamara was robbing the bank and now that she was a bit older and no longer penniless, that suited her quite well.

The problem was that Floyd Rasmussen was not a philosopher, but a crook. He was a man of quick changes. He loved his cat and all Disney movies. He also shot things for fun: deer, quail, even wildcats. Floyd turned on and off like a faucet which was levered by his own self-interest. She had liked Floyd in the beginning, though never quite enough to go to bed with him, as he had wanted. Now she wanted to see him dead.

And Threve? Thinking about Threve, Liz clutched her pillow spasmodically, hiding her face in white cotton. Threve was the devil himself. Without Threve, Rasmussen would be no threat to her, but Rasmussen himself was afraid of Threve.

Why? He wasn't much to look at. He was much shorter than Liz, and he dressed like a gigolo, raising eyebrows in the expensive places where he liked to spend his time. Being in Threve's company had been purgatory for Liz, but she had not dared avoid him, for fear of his temper. The three of them had been locked together in bonds of mutual guilt, in which camraderie soured into distrust.

She had spent much of her life in the company of people she didn't like and wasn't able to avoid. Her mother's friends, for example.

She remembered her early years with glass clarity. Her father had disappeared when she was six. For years she carried the notion—picked up God knows where, certainly not from her mother—that he'd been taken bodily into heaven. Mother had let her believe this; it was only when she discovered, overhearing a phone conversation, that he had cleaned out the savings before he left that she realized the truth.

Then came mother's odd jobs, playing Mendelssohn and Wagner for weddings, Cole Porter at the occasional bar mitzvah. *Night and Day, Lohingrin, Miss Otis Regrets* . . . Liz couldn't listen to any of them without a shudder. In no sort of music could she find pleasure.

Mother had to work nights, too, playing bass at the jazz cafe, and came home in the early morning, her clothes smelling of smoke and beer. Sometimes, when the babysitter didn't show, she had to go with her mother, and curl up on the table in the pantry off the kitchen, where the Chinese dishwasher would babble interminably in Cantonese, in which every syllable sounded like a threat to the child.

She held none of this against her mother. Mother had had no choice. She had worked like a dog, with help from no one.

The terrible, hurting love Liz felt for her mother welled up in her until she could hardly breath. That was why she couldn't be near Martha Macnamara: why she'd fled the length of the country to go to college and stayed away ever since. Mother was a noble cause continually being lost. Liz gasped and the bed rippled under her like a warm, maternal bosom.

Their years of life together had been marked by the constant parade of stray people through their apartment:

fruitarians, musicologists, women with shaved heads and
men with politics. These were all friends Mother picked
up along the way, indiscriminately—or chosen according
to standards known to no one else in the world but
Mother. There was the fat woman who had told Liz to
call her Bagheera, who slept on the zabutons in the
dining room for a week every summer. There was big,
smelly piper named Hamish who insisted on making his
instrument imitate a squealing pig, thinking to amuse
the little girl. Once, half by accident, she had referred to
him as Anus, causing her mother to drop a plate of
tomato slices on the kitchen floor. The memory nudged
Liz into smiling.

The one characteristic shared by all Mother's friends
was that they were irresistably attracted to Mother. They
came for her sudden blue flashes of insight, when she
would lift her head and point, speaking a few words to
prove she *did* understand what the speaker had been
saying in an hour's confused, monotonous monologue—
bursting the confusion with an arrow of pure good sense.

They came for the curve of her mother's neck
and her grace of movement. They came for lessons,
arrangements, transpositions, hamburgers . . . They
came with broken dreams, with fiddles unstrung, without carfare home . . .

Without exception they took more than they gave, and
Mother, who was a real musician—a professional, and a
real spiritual expert—a human being, allowed them to
play their games around her as if she were blind to them.

Liz's fists balled up in anger at people.

And Stanford she had found to be filled with the same
sort of self-involved zanies. They dressed badly, their
rooms reeked of dope, and they babbled interminably.
She had found that her fellow students were friendliest
when they were about to borrow money from her. In that
freshman year she had learned to protect herself from
leeches: deadbeats, grabby dates, "friends" who only
wanted to crib her papers. She became very good at it
and soon had few friends of any sort.

She'd envied the students in business administration. They got up in the morning at reasonable hours, dressed as well as their purses permitted, and studied with moderate diligence, knowing it would pay them in the end. Of course, these were a different breed, and in a way a lesser breed, for Liz was an engineer. But she followed the regimen as closely as her thirsty mind permitted.

When she had money, she would be able to call bullshit bullshit. When she had money, her mother would have time to be a real musician again—in concert halls instead of bars.

The contrast between the dream and reality drove a single cry from her throat. She flung herself to her feet.

There, in front of her eyes, lay Mayland Long's clothes, folded neatly. These were the only reassurances she had that the strange man had really been there—was actually out somewhere in the night trying to find her mother.

She touched the white shirt. By the dry, smooth feel of it, it was silk. The suit, too: raw silk, undyed. She called an image to mind and saw him again, standing composed and still in the doorway of the kitchen, holding the bottle aloft, like a lantern.

His manner, too, had been dry and smooth. She had fallen apart in front of him—a thing she had not done before any human being since coming to Stanford. She had offered to give him everything she had, and had meant it. She still meant it—money, reputation, flesh, future—all of it would be a good trade for the life of her mother. And he had turned the conversation gently aside.

She had the feeling that Mr. Long had refused her merely because he had all he could want or need already. It was all just the way he wanted it. Clothes, manner, confidence.

Yet this was the man Martha Macnamara had hired for a few thousand dollars. To risk his life.

Of course he liked Mother. That was clear from the

way he spoke about her. But everyone talked that way about Mother. Liz accepted that as her mother's due.

In the corner of her eye she saw movement—herself in the standing mirror. She did not like her body. It was awkward, and the bones were too big. She turned back to the folded shirt.

It was silk. It gave her hope.

11

The small cities of the Peninsula followed one another along the freeway. Mayland Long drove, his headlights cutting through a fog of pain. His single useable hand clutched the bottom of the wheel. The right arm lay limp, the hand resting on his thigh. At a dip in the road it shifted. This hurt so his grip on the wheel slid, and the Citroën veered across two lanes. Fortunately, his was the only car on the road.

The Rengstorff exit loomed ahead. He took the curve slowly, but was forced nonetheless against the door of the car. Wheels scraped gravel. The left side of the car dipped as it left the pavement, but he threw himself against the wheel and found the road again.

The Southern Pacific Railroad track rattled beneath his wheels. Only the forgiving suspension of the Citroën made the jolting bearable. He turned right on University Street and glided the car to a dark stop.

The building in which Threve lived sat amid grubby wooden houses like a stork in a pond full of ducks. The high-rise sparkled in the dim moonlight; its concrete facing had been mixed with glass. It was a white, impregnable virgin of a building, having no windows on the ground floor.

Long skirted the ghostly walls, treading the grass of its

tiny lawn. Wearily, he leaned against the bole of a small olive tree, his shape hidden by moonlight among silvery leaves. He no longer felt the cold.

There were two doors set into the rear face of the building. One of these was glass, and possessed a splended brass lock. The other was steel, with a lock to match. Mr. Long walked up to the glass door.

He needed his good hand, which had been supporting his wounded left arm. He forced his left hand into his jeans pocket.

Mr. Long knew a bit about metals. He believed he could force the aluminum frame of the door, even if the lock was too strong. Yet he stopped with his fingers wrapped around the door-pull, remembering his error at Rasmussen's house.

He investigated the other door. It smelled of garbage. This lock could not be forced, and though the idea of dismantling it appealed to Long's curiosity, he had neither tools nor time.

He turned the doorknob tentatively and the door opened. A wad of ancient gum was blocking the bolt-hole.

He found himself in a reeking chamber full of trash. He picked up a black plastic bag—one that upon inspection seemed less noisome than the rest—and proceeded through the inside door.

Threve's apartment number was 10-10. Long took the elevator; he could not have climbed the stairs. It was empty, and when the box stopped, he cradled the soft package against his chest and stepped into the hall.

"Stop!" cried the voice of a woman. "Hold it!" She wore nurse's whites. The "it" she referred to was the elevator. Mayland Long squeezed his burden higher, obscuring his face, and propped the door with his foot.

She had red hair. She smiled. "Thanks," she continued in more conventional tones. "Sorry 'bout the noise. I forget other people sleep nights." The doors closed and the kindly face vanished into the depths.

"Do they?" whispered Mr. Long to the empty hall.

Threve's apartment was at the end of the hall. Beside

the door Long dropped the small bag of trash; its function was fulfilled.

Speed was essential now, not stealth. Mayland Long meant to see Mr. Threve and to be seen by him. In heat of rage or chilly wet night, he would get answers from the hoodlum.

The door jamb of 10-10 snapped with a single explosive crack. He stepped in and pulled the door closed behind him.

The apartment was empty. He crept from the front room to the bedroom. He kicked open the door to the miniscule bathroom. Nothing. Finally he entered the kitchen, put his mouth beneath the tap and drank. He was a long time at it.

Now what? Should he wait for the unpleasant Mr. Threve to return? He could not wait long, for it was after midnight, and there was the matter of the letter to be accomplished. . . .

He busied himself as productively as he could, searching through Threve's belongings. Prying into the private affairs of others had always been one of Mr. Long's deepest interests, and now it served to distract his mind from his body's calamity.

Under the telephone in the bedroom he found an address book, old, spine-broken and filled with scraps of paper. He carried it out to the front room and began sifting through it, while listening for sounds from the elevator.

The oldest entries, judging by the fading of the ink, were of places in Detroit. Other cities were represented, notably Austin, Texas and Baton Rouge. Evidently, Mr. Threve was a traveler, and had only recently arrived in California. That was a help, for it reduced the number of relevant entries.

He sat upon a boxy white sofa beneath the large window of the living room. He read by the light of the full moon.

He placed his finger upon a promising scrap of paper,

then started at a glimpse of movement at the far end of the room.

He stood up and walked toward a figure which walked toward him. It was a shadowy man dressed in shapeless clothes, one hand stuck insolently in a pocket.

The entire wall of the room was covered with mirror panels. The image jumped and danced at the intersections of the squares. He stood respectfully in front of the image, as though he were waiting for it to speak to him, as though the faceless, sullen figure knew something he did not. His right hand folded the address in two and stuffed it away. The image then appeared with both hands in pockets, or possibly chained behind its back. It stood with its head down: a prisoner awaiting sentence. This sad figure was no one he knew.

Outside the broken door his odorous camouflage was waiting. He picked up the garbage bag and headed for the elevator. He knew his appearance would not stand up to much scrutiny; the rusty stains on his gray sweatshirt covered half its surface. The shirt was stiff and stuck to his back. He could smell the drying blood.

He was very warm, and with warmth came the desire for sleep. This desire was mitigated by the distant white dazzle of the moon. He heard the pounding again, but it seemed too slow to be his heartbeat. It was too much like the sea.

The engine turned over and the fan blasted hot air against his face. He turned it off.

He'd been driving all day and night, it seemed. He would need gas soon. He was losing his taste for driving.

The address in his pocket was not far: just across the line into Sunnyvale. He drove down the empty El Camino, straight at the moon.

The building was nothing more than a concrete shed, surrounded by gravel. The immediate area was zoned for industry, and was desolate by night. The words *Rasmussen Mos* were painted in orange letters across the front wall, but it appeared the place had passed beyond that particular incarnation. Mallow and dock grew among the stones of the parking lot, and the shriveled heads of chickweed made a desolate border beneath the wall. It seemed to be one of Rasmussen's earlier miscalculations—if in truth his bankruptcies had been accidental.

No cars were to be seen. The two doors of the building were green steel. There were no windows.

No noise leaked out, even when he put his ear to the metal. He sighed and leaned against the door, summoning what remained of his strength.

There were tracks in the gravel, from a vehicle which had driven right up to the door and backed away again. No telling how long the tracks had been there.

The factory was a fortress, but Mr. Long was not overawed by fortresses. He closed his eyes, seized the knob, and pulled.

The knob came out in his hand, trailing its tarnished entrails. The sliding bolt fell into the round hole the knob had left, and the door creaked open; the deadbolt had not been set.

He stepped into a wide empty room, lit only by the light emanating from a gaping refrigerator. The room held one wooden table, gouged and solder stained, a filthy white folding chair and a litter of magazines. Approaching closer he found in one corner more magazines that had been arranged into three piles, one pile four inches high and the other two consisting of one *Playboy* and one *Dr. Dobb's* each, with the computer journal on top. These three piles made a triangle eighteen inches on a side. Next to this formation was the sad carcass of a tape recorder, smashed. Within it he could see a small white cassette tape. Mayland Long would have given much to know what was on that tape. He put it in his pocket.

Prowling the perimeter of the room, he came to the open refrigerator. He felt within it.

The shelves were still cold. His breath drew in in a long hiss.

Continuing his investigation, he found the bathroom

by the back door. He entered and turned on the light.
The bottom of the sink was damp.

On the bathroom wall, amid graffiti in English and
Spanish, someone had drawn a large red circle. It began
and ended at the top. It was a fat, open, hearty circle,
drawn in fresh lipstick. In Zen Buddhist tradition it
meant nothing. Literally nothing—zero, Mu, the Void.
To Mr. Long it meant quite a lot.

He staggered into the yard, scattering gravel. He
leaned his back against the door of the car. Trying to
untangle his keys from the cassette tape, he dropped
both on the roadway. He stooped for them, and found
himself on hands and knees on the concrete, overcome
by the knowledge of failure. He cried out, a thin,
wordless, wail.

Too late . . . Too slow . . . Too late . . .

Breathing raggedly, he found the keys, the tape. He
climbed to his feet and stood motionless for sixty
seconds.

He got in the car.

The knocking continued. Fred crawled out of bed,
dazed. The clock said 2:45.

This was a real bitch.

He slept in his b.v.d.'s, and wearing nothing else he
stood by the door.

"Whozat?" he croaked, his voice breaking in the
middle of the compound word.

"Frisch? Fred. It's Mayland Long. I hope you remember me."

Had Frisch forgotten the name, he could not have
forgotten the voice. He wrestled with the lock and flung
the door open. Long stepped in.

"Forgive me. I am aware of the hour. I have come
because I need your help, Fred. Both the Macnamara
women are in terrible danger, and I know no one else to
whom I can go."

Frisch blinked and stared. "You're white as a sheet,"
was all he found to say. "Sit down."

"Am I?" whispered Mr. Long, obeying. "How odd. I thought there was nothing white about me." Suddenly he started up again. "I will ruin your upholstery."

"Too late for that," mumbled Frisch. "Years too late." He squatted on the floor next to Long, taking the blood-stiffened fabric in his hands.

"What in hell happened to you?"

The wounded man gently pulled the shirt out of Frisch's grip. "I've been shot in the shoulder. Please don't."

Frisch sat back on his haunches. "You gotta go to the hospital, man. I'll drive you."

"No. I don't have the time. Martha Macnamara has been kidnapped by men who intend to kill her. I must forge a letter on a RasTech text processor—an 8080—and hand it to Elizabeth before tomorrow morning."

"You can't do anything if you bleed to death," insisted Frisch, letting the rest of the statement slide by him. He dropped his hands to his knees and stood up. He headed for the bathroom.

"The bleeding has stopped, I think," replied Mr. Long. "And I cannot use the machine at all, which is why I came to you."

Frisch came back with a pair of shears. He knelt again beside Long. The heavy blades sliced through the fabric of the sweatshirt.

"I was a boy scout. Got a first aid merit badge." He cut from the waistband to the neck while the older man watched. Silver blades gnashed together, but slowly their bright surfaces grew dull, as though with rust. When Frisch began snipping through the left sleeve, Long gasped and swayed. Frisch apologized, but kept cutting.

The cloth at the top of the shoulder was stuck to the wound. Frisch cut around it, and the remains of the gray sweatshirt fell to the cushions of the chair.

Fred Frisch whistled. "Oooh, man. You ought to see your side."

"I can do without."

Frisch dropped his scissors on the worn carpet. "Who shot you?"

Long leaned back. "Floyd Rasmussen. With some sort of hunting rifle." His eyes glittered. He rubbed at them. "I didn't know a gun could make so little noise."

Mr. Long was not really white, but he was decidedly gray against Frisch's decrepit green recliner chair. His eyes fell shut. He heard Frisch in the distance, along with the sound of running water.

"It is hot in here," he observed. "I imagined the rain would cool the air."

Agony struck him in the shoulder, worse than the pain of the bullet. Long grabbed at the source of it.

Frisch gasped and cried out. A steaming cloth dropped onto Long's lap.

"Leggo!" cried Frisch. "Let go. Please! You're breaking my arm!"

Astonished, Long released him. "I'm so very sorry," he said. "I didn't know what you were doing."

The young blond flexed his fingers doubtfully. "Good God, Mr. Long. Where did you develop a grip like that?"

"I didn't develop it. Holding on comes naturally to me." He tried to smile. "But I won't do it again, I promise."

Frisch soaked the cloth again. "It's going to hurt just as bad," he warned his patient. He lowered the washcloth onto the filthy wound.

As he had promised, Long did not attack Frisch. He passed out.

12

Fred continued soaking the wound in warm water laced with Betadine. At length the mangled scrap of fabric came off. The exit hole of the bullet was black and ragged, though it had not adhered to the shirt. He put his hand behind Long's back and eased the man forward, propping him with a sofa cushion.

With every unconscious twitch of his patient Fred flinched. The tendons along his forearm still hurt when he clenched his hand. Jeezus what kind of grip this guy had . . . Must have been adrenaline, like with the little kids who pull cars off their mothers . . .

He ought to call the police. This guy was in no shape to tackle anything more tonight. Kidnapping. Attempted murder.

Maybe this Mr. Long was simply a lunatic. Maybe the story he told Fred at the shop was sheer gas—after all, the woman who came with him, with her ballerina hair, the one he said was Liz Macnamara's mother, hadn't followed the conversation. And she had seemed a bit happy herself.

But who shoots a lunatic in the shoulder? And from above. Top down. Was Rasmussen sitting in a tree when he shot Mr. Long?

He did not really doubt his visitor's story. He only wished that he could. And he thought he really ought to call the police.

What he did instead was to dribble hydrogen peroxide into both bullet wounds. He winced as he watched the stuff foam. Long's lips pulled back from his teeth but his eyes did not open. He noticed the teeth—white, perfect and heavily rooted. He always noticed teeth; he had spent four years in orthodontia.

He went rummaging through the medicine cabinet. Not finding all he wanted, he proceeded through the kitchen drawers. Finally he raided his tool box.

The red wounds he covered with gauze pads, which he attached by adhesive tape. The damaged arm he bent at the elbow and lay flat against his patient's stomach, securing it with duct tape wrapped around the body.

He stepped back and examined his handiwork.

Serviceable. No design award, but the guy looked better than he had before. Except for his color, which was bad.

With a great deal of trepidation, he bent down and raised Mr. Long, one hand under the knees and the other at the shoulders. The task was far easier than he'd feared. Mr. Long was very light.

Maybe he had hollow bones. Why not? He looked strange enough in other respects. Those hands, for instance.

Maybe he was an extraterrestrial, passing for human. An extraterrestrial detective. From Fomalhaut, maybe. And Rasmussen was the most-wanted criminal in this arm of the galaxy. He liked this idea. He could relate to it more easily than that of someone kidnapping Liz Macnamara. Or was it her mother that was kidnapped?

He lowered Long to the carpet, gently. Next he yanked all the back cushions from the couch and stuffed them under his patient's knees. He wondered if Long were a marathon racer and that was why he was so light and strong. He himself jogged.

He went into his bedroom and pulled the blanket off the bed. Kneeling beside the sick man he hesitated, blanket in hand. He put his hand on the tight dry skin of the man's forehead.

Jeez, he was hot . . . Really burning up. He didn't need a blanket; he needed icepacks.

He needed a hospital. Fred wavered in indecision while his hand—which was like all of him, rather chilly in the air of night—moved to the back of Long's neck. He felt tension harden the muscles before he saw the brown eyes open.

"How did I get here?" Mr. Long inquired mildly.

"Oh. Well, you looked kinda bad, and I remembered from boy scouts 'Face red, raise the head. Face pale, raise the tail.' "

"A useful maxim, but inelegant," the dark man whispered. Long looked about him, noticing the shabby furnishings, the worn rug, the piles of incomprehensible electronics equipment gathered in the corners of the room like dust kitties and sharing the surface of the single table with two pears and a loaf of Orowheat Brand bread. None of the machines seemed to be in working order, judging by the bouquets of bell wire and brass popping from the tops or seams, the black holes where knobs should have been, the green boards protruding at odd angles from the frames . . .

"What time is it?" Long asked. Among all this mechanical litter, there was no clock to be seen.

Fred trotted into the bedroom. "Three-twenty," he called back. When he returned to the living room Long was standing.

"I have no more time, Fred. I thank you for what you have done. Will you also do what I asked of you?"

Under the intensity of Long's gaze Fred was aware of his near-nakedness. He shifted from one bare foot to the other. "Can't we call the police?"

"When we have the letter we can call the police. The letter may become my bargaining power with Rasmussen and his colleague. I found where they were keeping Martha Macnamara, but they had moved her before I arrived."

"That might mean . . . that . . . I mean . . ."

"That she is dead? It might, but I don't think so." Long

did not explain further. Instead he added, "I have no way
to find her. I don't believe the police would be in a better
state. Only Rasmussen or Threve can lead me to Martha
now, and I may need that letter for bait.

"If you don't want to become involved I will return to
Elizabeth's apartment and waylay the hoodlums as they
arrive."

"You will? You can barely stand up!" cried Frisch.

Mr. Long's lips parted with a trace of a smile. Frisch
glimpsed those teeth, and with a chaining of memory he
touched his aching right arm.

"Acrobatics may not be necessary," said Long. "But I
can't blame you for not wanting to . . . to delve into
this affair. It is dangerous and of disputable legality. And
you have already ruined a night's sleep to help a man
who has no claim upon you . . ."

"Wait a minute. I never *said* I didn't want to help you
with this letter business. All I'm saying is . . ." Fred
looked about him. His blond moustache whuffled with
the force of his thoughts. His hands lifted from his sides
and slapped down again, helplessly. ". . . is . . .

"Let me get some clothes on. That's all."

"Some car!"

Mayland Long accepted the tribute with a nod.
"There are not many of them in California. Never until
tonight have I been so glad of the automatic transmission." He lowered himself slowly into the driver's seat.
He was now wearing a red flannel shirt of Fred's, soft and
blouselike, which fit easily over the taped arm. The
empty sleeve was tucked into the waistband of his Levis.
He caught a glimpse of himself in the mirror.

"I look like a one-armed lumberjack."

Fred had remained standing by the door, leaning into
the open window. "No way," he stated. He sought for
words to explain how very difficult it would be for Mr.
Long to look like a lumberjack. "No way," he repeated.

"Maybe I better drive, huh?"

"No," said Long. The word came out sounding like the answer to a question rather than the blunt refusal it was. He waited for Frisch to get in.

"So tell me," urged the young man. "What's the story? Why is Floyd Rasmussen going around kidnapping people and zapping them with guns?"

Long told the story. He told it not from the viewpoint of his own involvement, but chronologically, beginning with the affair of Carlo Peccolo and Liz Macnamara and her subsequent disillusionment, and leading up to the finding of the smashed tape recorder and the circle on the wall of the bathroom. He spoke so that Frisch should know the sort of trouble he was purchasing, but in his words the explanation became a tale of blood and betrayal.

Frisch sat gaping when Long was done. "Jeezus. What made Liz *do* such a stupid thing?"

Long grunted and licked his cracked lips. "I believe she wanted to become a wizard. That is what she said, at least."

"Oof!" Frisch stretched in his seat and cracked his knuckles behind his head. "Everyone wants to be a wizard. Every engineer, that is. Goes with unicorns and dragons: but with technical people it's particularly wizards—a secret fantasy that lies behind all the pin diagrams. It's really silly, don't you know? Wizards! But engineers can be really naive about themselves; they think because they can design a pc board and it's right and it works, that everything they do or believe is going to be just that right. Better than what the nerd on the street does or believes. That's where wizards come in. Secret ways. Secret knowledge. Not bound by ordinary rules. Liz is a little bit like that, isn't she?"

Long smiled ruefully. "She did want to be a wizard," he admitted. "So unlike her mother."

Fred nodded his understanding. "I myself try not

to . . . not to take myself too seriously, you know? But I get into it too: working at night, with all the colored lights blinkin', and the machine responding to my commands.

"It's all a power trip, man." Frisch settled into himself, chewing on his moustache as the car sped on. The moon was now directly overhead.

Long's voice broke the stillness. "I see. That explains wizards. What about unicorns?"

This question was not easy for the engineer to answer. "I dunno. I heard they were symbols of virginity, hundreds of years ago. Nobody I know goes in for virginity."

Long laughed, and bright wheels of pain formed in his shoulder. His mind was clouding over. He sought to keep Frisch talking. "Dragons?"

"Power." Frisch spoke with decision. "Raw power."

"Is that all?" asked Mayland Long. "Is that all there is to dragons?"

"Isn't that enough? Terror on bat wings. Fire and cold stone. Gold and jewels in heaps. Raw power!" He paused for only a moment. "Watch out when you meet a guy on a dragon trip!"

Mr. Long spared a moment from the road to glance at Fred Frisch, who sat, hands laced behind his neck, pale hair waving to his shoulders.

That rosy face shone like an angel's in the moonlight. He was no more than a boy. Long felt himself buffeted by the cruelties of time. He spoke.

"In China, it was different. I think. Chinese dragons were not always such brutes. They lived for centuries, and had a certain reputation for wisdom."

Frisch brought his hands down. "Didn't they eat people?"

Long grinned. "At times. And at times people ate dragons. Powdered dragon's blood has been known to bring a man back from the edge of death."

Frisch looked doubtfully at Mr. Long. "Are you
. . . Chinese?" he asked.

"More or less." Long strangled a yawn, afraid how the
movement would affect his shoulder. His face was hot
and dry. His lip was bleeding.

"The Chinese imperial dragon has five toes to a foot.
All others have three or four."

"Why's that such a difference?"

"It makes it much easier for him to turn the pages of
books. To write letters to his friends," answered Mayland Long.

"Don't laugh. It is true."

To their surprise the building which housed RasTech
was lit and open. A small circle of men squatted on the
front stoop, drinking soda and tossing pennies. Long and
Frisch hesitated at the foot of the walk.

"This is an additional complication," whispered Long.

"I guess somebody in there works three shifts. 'Can't
believe it's RasTech. Those guys look like Mexicans.
Probably they do parts assembly."

"One of them is Mexican born." The sick man spoke
absently. "The rest seem to be from the Central Valley,
by their accent.

"But their presence, and that of the guard in the
lobby, forces me to rethink our strategy. I'd planned to
break the lock."

"Well, now we won't have to," replied Fred Frisch,
and he skipped bouyantly toward the door.

Mr. Long followed.

The guard was tan faced, portly and balding. As the
two entered he put down a Harlequin romance. Fred
was a vision of blond innocence. He sailed to a stop
before the guard and leaned over the desk.

"I'm supposed to meet Floyd Rasmussen here," he
said. "I'm a little late."

The fat man blinked. His English was not too good.

"No Mister Rasmussen here. Not in the night. Come back tomorrow."

Fred ran his hand through his hair. "We have to boot up the system. *Comprende?* Boot up the system?"

"Do you want me to translate?" murmured Long in Fred's ear.

"No," answered Fred in the same tones. "I want him to stay confused."

The guard cleared his throat and glanced wistfully at his book. "Booting is not my business. Come back tomorrow."

"But if we don't boot the system right now, it's going to get hot for us. Overheat. *Muy caliente* and a lot of money."

The guard's pudgy face creased with worry, but he shrugged. "I cannot boot: What can I do?"

"You have the keys, I know. Let us in so we can do it."

The guard blinked resentfully. "I cannot do that," he stated. "It is not permitted."

Fred ran both his hands through his hair and his moustache bristled like a live thing. "Have you ever seen a computer crash?" he demanded. "It's horrible. All over the floor! It will put Rasmussen out of business."

Unhappily, the guard stood. He looked vaguely around, as though the corners of the lobby could give him some advice. He put his hand into his baggy uniform pocket and pulled out a ring of keys.

"You come," he commanded, with great bitterness. "When you leave, I have to search you."

"Fair enough," said Fred, as the private door opened before them. Long withheld comment.

13

In Rasmussen's office, lit only by window light, the model of the ship cast complex shadows on the floor. Fred bent to marvel at the miniature while Mayland Long perused the wall of yellowed comic strips, studying the tastes of this man who had come so near to killing him.

He liked *Hagar the Horrible*, evidently, and a strip titled *Garfield*. Anything by Kliban. Anything with cats.

Long remembered the wretched cry of the white cat in the bathroom. The cat had betrayed him to Rasmussen—by accident, of course. He had, in turn, caused the cat's death.

Also by accident.

Rasmussen's taste was pedestrian—nothing in the decoration of this wall exposed the humorist as a murderer. But then, Mayland Long could also laugh. And kill men.

He leaned against the wall, waiting for Frisch to be done. It was hard to stand. Swallowing, too, was becoming difficult.

"This is a beauty. You like boats?" called Fred.

"No."

The weariness expressed in a single syllable brought the young man out of his reverie.

"Sorry," he said, peering through the dark. "I'll look for the system now."

Mr. Long followed Fred Frisch from room to room, searching for anything which resembled a microprocessor with printer connections. It was not easily found. After a few minutes, Long realized his efforts were hindering the search. He returned to the reception room and sank into the secretary's swivel chair.

At least with the lights out one did not notice that the walls were orange. The flat telephone console was green, however, as was the terminal screen at the secretary's desk. Evidently this was a "paperless" office, such as Long had read about in the pages of *EDN* magazine. That meant that all correspondence was stored on disk and sent to the printer as copies were desired.

He tried to call Fred; his voice failed him. On the second try he succeeded.

Frisch appeared. Long pointed to the box in front of him. "Is this a microprocessor?"

Fred smote his forehead with the heel of his hand. "What a jerk I am! Here I am, clawing my way through the back labs looking for something esoteric and here it is.

"Sure. The box is a Vector—that's 8080 all right, and the rest of the system . . . well I don't know."

Long eased out of the chair. "I had hoped you would know."

"Nope." Fred explored the desk with nimble fingers, searching for the various power switches.

"Will you be able to use it?"

"Dunno that either," grunted Fred, offhand. A fan began to whirr. After five minutes he succeeded in lighting the screen with gibberish.

A harsh, rattling sigh reached Fred's ears. He swiveled in the chair.

What he saw broke through his concentration. Long was crouching on the carpet behind the desk. His knees were up and his head rested between them. His usable arm encircled his legs and his left hand hung limp, trembling visibly.

With a squeal of chair wheels, Fred got up. He stepped awkwardly over to Long and laid his own hand on the glossy black hair. "Don't worry," he said. "When I said I didn't know how, that didn't mean I couldn't learn. I'm pretty good at this impromptu kind of thing.

"And you know what they say. 'If you know what you're doing, it isn't research.' "

Long lifted his head. His eyes were faceted with gold. Fred smiled.

"Ignore my noises. It's only that I'm losing my voice," rasped Long. Suddenly his eyebrows lifted and he added, "Mr. Frisch, you are stuffed like a sausage full of little sayings."

Fred laughed. "Surprise you to learn that I've read *Don Quixote*, too. I always thought I'd make a good Sancho Panza." He brushed off his knees and returned to the console.

"Actually, I'm not entirely your typical North Californian, with head carved out of redwood burl. You know, 'Nuke the Whales' bumper sticker, doing yoga suspended in a vat of blood-temperature salts." Fred typed as he talked, trying to establish some sort of rapport with the green box.

"I'm not even from California. But then who is? I'm a good half-Jewish boy from Shaker Heights, Ohio. I've been afraid to tell my friends here, but I don't believe in reincarnation."

Fred scowled and backed his chair away. "This isn't working. I don't think the bootstrap is in ROM at all. Who, this day and age, would be so clunky as to . . ."

His quick eye covered the desk, the table set against it, the file cabinets along the wall. Finally he noticed a box the size of a toaster covered by an embroidered cozy which read "Bless this Mess." With a flourish he yanked off the cover, revealing a paper-tape reader with a neat row of spools built into the front.

"White ribbons! What a sight. Now we're cookin' with gas." He held up to the light three of the wound tapes. He chose the smudgiest and inserted that into the machine, nudging on the power and the read switch. Immediately the strip of paper tape shot through the slit in the machine and appeared at the other side. Fred waltzed back to the chair in time to receive the message PANDEMANIC WORD PROCESSING SYSTEM FILE MANAGER AND EDITOR PROGRAM v. 1.0. Without pause words INPUT TIME AND DATE (24 HR CLOCK) AS FOLLOWS: MM/DD/YY/.HH/MM.

Fred crowed his triumph, then settled down to interrogate the system. After a few minutes, he turned to find Long sprawled on the floor, asleep.

"I wish I didn't have to wake you, friend," he muttered. "You've had just as hard a time as a man can take. I think your line of work must be all nails and no shoe leather. But then, that's the way it is for most people, I guess. Too much silly work, dull or dangerous, and not enough dough.

"I'm damn lucky for a punk kid."

Fred swiveled back to the screen. "Maybe I don't have to wake you up, yet. Le'me see if I can find the library, here . . ." He typed a few questions and the answers pleased him.

"I run, you know," whispered Fred to the sleeper. "More to clear my head after work than for macho. I go from the park by Menlo City Hall down along the tracks to Stanford. Down by the railroad bridge there's a tree that Palo Alto was named for: 'the big stick.' Everybody around here knows about that tree, but no one stops to see it—at least I never see anybody there but me.

"I'm not a very type-A guy, you know? Not driven. I stop and touch the tree everytime I go by, and if I'm winded I give it a big sweaty hug and lean against it a while. It's the oldest live thing around here. Must be five hundred years."

Another flurry of key-strikes and the screen filled with print. Fred scrolled it slowly.

"I don't have a philosophy about it, or anything like that, but I think there's a peace around old things. You can feel it. If you get close, you can share it."

"To be old is not always a guarantee of peace," answered a dry, snakeskin voice behind him. Startled, Fred spun around.

"I'm sorry. I was mostly talking to myself," he said. Mr. Long was attempting to sit up. His face was pale and brilliant. Fred leaned over to forestall him.

"Not yet. Give me a few more minutes. But we're in the groove, here, so you just rest. I'll wake you if I need you."

He returned to his work. Almost immediately he found what he had been looking for. He cuffed the console affectionately.

"Besides, I meant really old things—not old as a man can get old, but old like a tree. Hundreds of years."

"I am a very old worm," sighed Mayland Long, his fevered eyes gazing at the ceiling. "I have been searching for an illusive nothing called truth. Now I think I would settle for sleep, if I had the choice."

Fred had been following with half an ear. He worried he would have to carry Long back to the car. "For a worm, I'm sure you'd be positively geriatric. But forty-five, fifty, whatever—isn't what I'd call old. And you're perfectly welcome to catch some zees now, Mr. Long. We're safe, and the machine is eating out of my hand."

He hit carriage return, and the discreet hiss of an ink jet printer sounded in the corner of the office. He rose, stretched, and cracked his knuckles.

Next to the printer stood a coffee vending machine. Fred dug into his pocket for money. He returned to Mr. Long with a steaming plastic cup in his hand.

"Here you go. Empty calories." He proffered the cup. "Say. I don't know what to call you. I mean, I *can* call you Mister Long all the livelong night, but it feels awkward, not knowing the rest. Is Long your Chinese name?"

Mr. Long sat up and reached for the cup. His hand shook as he took it. After the first sip he blinked in surprise. "What is this?"

"Cocoa."

"Ah." Long held it in both hands. "My—Chinese name is simply Oolong. I use a first name, which is a Latin translation on the original. Or it was; it's been corrupted through the years." He coughed, and chocolate splashed on the rug. Fred steadied the cup with one hand.

"Translation. That's interesting. What does the name mean, then?"

Mayland Long smiled at Fred. "I hesitate to tell you, after our conversation in the car. Oolong has two meanings. It means a kind of tea, and it means black dragon.

"But I assure you, Fred; I did not name myself."

Fred hit his forehead once again. "I gotta big mouth. Forget what I said in the car. I don't know beans about China. Drink."

Fred tore off the listing and began to read. His interest grew. Long stood, using the wall for support. "What is that?"

"The letter."

The dark man walked slowly over, his brow furrowed . . . "I don't remember dictating it. Have I been so ill . . ."

"It was on disk," replied Fred Frisch. "She left it sitting in the secretary's library and no one thought to look. Not even the secretary." He handed the scroll of paper to the other, commenting, "It's fascinating. She names dates, places and amounts of withdrawal. She's got an orderly mind."

Long read. He nodded in agreement.

"Liz and I were in all the same classes when we were frosh. I had this huge crush on her," Fred blurted.

Mr. Long looked up from the page he was reading. "I see. She didn't return the sentiment?"

"Naw. She was after bigger fish."

"She told you so?"

Fred scratched his head. He blushed. "I never told her about it. No use."

Long regarded him intently. "So that's why you agreed to help me."

The blond youth returned the stare. "No. No, I don't think that's why. I—I think I mean don't you think I'd do it just because . . ." He broke off and began the ritual of powering down the equipment.

Mayland Long finished the letter in silence.

The guard patted each of Frisch's pockets before standing aside. Then he approached Long, who stared down at the fat man from infinite heights. "*Yo no tengo nada*," he said.

For five seconds they locked eyes. "*Lo creo*," muttered the guard finally, and he ambled back to his desk and to romance.

The sky had returned crystalline while Frisch was working. A late night wind struck their faces and made streamers of their steaming breaths. Mr. Long inhaled deeply.

"I feel tremendously better, Fred. The cocoa was a saving grace."

Fred Frisch strode ahead and reached the Citroën before Long. He stood with legs braced in front of the driver's door. "Let me drive."

Mr. Long shook his head. "This car is very complex."

Frisch stood firm. "Remember me? I'm the quick study."

"Don't you trust my driving?" Long's voice was lightly ironical.

Frisch's answer was not. "No. You're sick, and there's enough danger in this whole business without me worrying about going into the median strip or ending my life plowing into the front grill of someone else's Volkswagon."

Long extended the keys to Frisch. "You're right, of course." He walked around the car.

Fred Frisch felt obscurely guilty as he studied the

instrument board. The automatic hydraulic suspension levitated the body of the car as the engine caught; Fred had heard about the strange Citroën suspension, but this was his first experience driving it. At least the controls appeared familiar. He played out the clutch gently, experimenting.

Mr. Long loosened his grip on the dash. "You *are* a quick study," he commented. "I expected rather a rougher start."

Frisch shrugged. "Where do we go now?" he asked. "We?"

"Of course we. You don't think I can go back to sleep after all this, do you Mister Dragon?"

Long's smile grew and deepened into laughter. "Fred! Have you such an appetite for adventure? But I forget— I'm talking to a young man. Let's return to your apartment, for now. I must make a telephone call."

"To call who?"

"I will tell you when we get there."

Fred looked at the clock. "It's just after four. You say Liz is safe until the banks open?"

"I hope so. Until Rasmussen and Threve believe they have the incriminating letter, they dare not kill the daughter."

"But what about . . . Mrs. Macnamara?"

Mr. Long's answer was slow in coming. "She is in terrible danger. The only reason they have for keeping her alive is that she can be used to pressure the daughter. If they believe this is not necessary, or if Martha refuses—has refused—to be so used, then they can be expected to kill her. And after they are done with her, they *must* kill her. She is a curious, sharp woman who has probably seen at least one of them face to face. How can they let her live?"

Fred's face clouded over, remembering the blue dress and the graying hair, and how the little voice-operated race car made circles on the floor. It was the sort of happening he fostered in his shop. That's what the shop was for: friendly computers. Friendly people.

"Can't the police help?" he asked.

"How? Tell me how, Fred, and I will show up on the precinct house doorstep with you. I cannot find Rasmussen or Threve . . ."

"Threve I never heard of. What does he look like?"

"Like Satan himself, I gather. Elizabeth fears him more than she does Rasmussen. Other than that, I know only that he is rather short and dresses loudly.

"I believe he drives a black Lincoln. At least I suspect such a car was involved with the kidnapping, and I didn't see it parked at RasTech. With no more information than this, can the police find Martha Macnamara?

"That is, can they find her in time? I am sure they would eventually turn up the body."

Frisch shuddered. "Jeez! Do you get hardened to things like this?"

"Do I?" inquired Long. "The longer one lives, the more one sees, it is true, but I don't feel hardened. Quite the contrary, in my youth I was far more . . . brutal."

"Then you're in the wrong line of work," insisted Fred. "No offense. I think a guy who could thrive in such a slimy world, with fraud and criminals, always a bit to the windward of the law . . . he'd have to be kind of a snake."

Long leaned over curiously. "What are you talking about, Fred. Which world is this?"

"I mean the world of ᴜᵤe private investigator. Or police investigator. Any detective."

"Ah." Mr. Long digested this, and began again to laugh, ignoring the lancing pain in his shoulder. "You believe I'm a private detective."

"You're not?" Fred's eyes darted wildly from the road to the smiling, tired face beside him. "Then what—who are you? How'd you get involved in this?"

Mr. Long sighed. "Starting with *what* I am: my field was languages, but I am now retired. *Who* is equally easy to explain. I am a friend of Martha Macnamara's.

How? Easiest of all. I promised her I would find her daughter.

"So you see. You have been aiding a bumbling amateur to trespass and steal documents. Have you second thoughts?"

Fred was staunch. "Jeez, no. I'm glad. I mean, there's something seamy about carrying the banner for money."

"But, Martha. Mrs. Macnamara. I'm really sorry. She seemed like a fine lady."

"No eulogies yet, please," growled Long. "I don't believe her to be dead. Allow me that."

The car glided to a stop in front of Frisch's duplex. He left it double parked. Both men got out.

Fred felt the keys of the car being pried from his hand. Half-embarrassed at his earlier show of force, he let them go and fumbled for his door key.

With the front door open, he turned to perceive that Mr. Long was not with him, but was unlocking the Citroën from the driver's side. Fred sprinted across the lawn.

"What're you doing?" he protested. "Trying to chuck me?"

"Yes, Fred. That is exactly it," Long admitted, gently fending the young man off. "I had hoped you would not be so quick."

"You can't do it. I won't let you go alone!"

Long placed his right hand on Frisch's shoulder. It was an affectionate, avuncular gesture and Frisch found he could not move at all. "You can hardly stop me, Fred."

Fred fought against Long's grip. Defeated, he tried words again. "If you leave me behind, I'll call the police."

The dark man turned his face away and the hand slipped off. "I can't prevent that," he admitted. "Not without harming or detaining you.

"And I won't do that." He slid into the seat.

Fred wedged himself between the door and frame. "But you need me. There are two baddies, and you have only one arm."

"Acrobatics may not be necessary," repeated Mr. Long.

"But they may. I may make a little bit of difference. Maybe the difference between saving a life and . . . and not. I may be very important." The young blond clutched at the door. His pale hair gleamed under the streetlight.

"You *are* very important, Fred," whispered Mayland Long. "And that is why I will not take you any further into this."

With a slow, irresistible pressure, he forced Frisch out into the street.

14

Martha Macnamara's universe was compassed by the groan and creak of wood, and by the chill of wet air. Had she been able to think, her very sickness might have convinced her she was still alive. She was denied that comfort, being barely conscious, and her thoughts were bound up with a rhythmic rise and sinking. The beat was *molto lento*, and she should be doing something in time with it. What?

That question gnawed at her. She tried breathing in time with the measure—no go. You can't force your breathing, she reminded herself. What then—sing? She couldn't remember a song as ponderous as the rhythm the world now kept, and she couldn't find her mouth anyway.

Neither could she find her hands, so she couldn't play the fiddle.

The staccato beat of footsteps superimposed itself over the slow rocking. She attended to the footsteps. Good.

Percussion rounded out the work nicely. Someone was taking care of things.

Martha was content.

He was driving on the reserve tank. That was unfortunate, but not to be helped, at this hour of the morning. Perhaps he could siphon gas from Elizabeth Macnamara's car.

As he had told Fred, he was feeling much better. This hideous night was falling behind him.

Something else, too, was falling behind: a danger or misery he could feel but to which he could put no name.

Perhaps it was despair.

He had partially fulfilled his promises, but promises were no longer the only things keeping him alive.

He felt the pressure of the sun's approach, as it ate up the night to the east. In two hours it would rise over California. The sun had always been a great source of comfort to him.

Yet he owed his increase in strength not to the slow roll of time, but to the spontaneous kindness of Fred Frisch. Except for the young engineer, he would probably not have survived. He felt the wonder of that charity shimmering within his mind.

Long could be compassionate, in his dry, reserved fashion. He had once or twice donated his varied and considerable strengths to the service of others. But he had rarely been subject to the compassion of mankind. He had rarely needed it.

And Frisch's response to a man who was almost a stranger went beyond casual kindness. He had given up sleep and ruined his furniture. Long injured the man's arm, and still he continued to help him. He risked jail. He offered to risk his life. How could Long comprehend such kindness, let alone pay it back? Like music, Frisch's gift to him could not be translated into terms of gain or loss. Nor was it subject to reason. It had no meaning but that of its own existence.

Idly, because he was a methodical creature who did

think in terms of gain and loss, Long began to tally the losses and gains of the last few days: loss of power. Loss of blood. Loss of new hope.

Loss of certainty.

On the credit side was only this encounter with an absurd young man who gave up a night's rest for Mayland Long. Who performed the onerous duties of a nurse. Who lent him a shirt.

Who dared place his hand on Long's head, and tell him it was all okay.

With a ledger like this, Mr. Long wondered, why did he feel so much stronger, now, driving toward the dawn?

The Citroën darted onto the freeway and he was pressed against the back of the seat. This was the last short step of the night's journey—to Elizabeth Macnamara's apartment. It would be profoundly anticlimactic if he ran out of gas.

The chill of the air prophesied fog later, but now, in the last hours of night, the sky was sharp and clear. He shifted in the seat, and his flannel shirt stuck to the leather upholstery, glued with drying blood.

At least this shirt was the right color.

He left the freeway and zagged right onto Middlefield. His arm was numb to the turn. Passing by Liz's condominium he noticed a single light shone yellow. He turned the corner and parked along a side street. He wondered if the car would start again. No matter. He would not be driving again soon.

A stone tower obscured the light of the stars. He had parked in front of a church. He was a connoisseur of all stone architecture, and churches in particular were his passion, but this edifice was disappointing. It was obviously new, and the stone was merely veneer. *TRINITY PARIS* read the signboard. A pale phantom *H* in the varnish at the end of the word marked where the brass letter had been lost.

He stood on the cold grass and yawned. "*De profundis clamor ad te,*" he growled to the cross on the empty tower—"Out of the depths a call to you." He was not certain to whom he was speaking. The effort made him cough. He moved away from the street, crossing through the churchyard.

The direction of his progress was against the clock, or widdershins. To cross a churchyard widdershins is not auspicious, as he knew, but in the churchyard of Trinity Parish no one was buried. All the ground was paved over by concrete.

Behind the church lot stood a hedge of yew. He passed through the omen of its furry branches and found himself beside a noise of waters. The fountain was lit from below, and its shower sprang up in an arcing circle to fall again with silver lights upon the backs of sleeping seagulls.

Cold spray beaded on his face. He stepped among the gulls, who stood on one leg or with head under wing, and they did not stir. He circled the fountain, avoiding light, and reached the white stone walk which wound between the gleaming buildings. No sound came from within the condominiums, not even the mumble of television. He came to Liz Macnamara's residence and stood beneath the window he had climbed through earlier in the evening.

Had it been just this evening?

The window was still open. Good. Had Elizabeth closed it he would not have been able to make the ascent. Not with one arm.

Drink, sleep or pray, he had said. According to your nature. What was Elizabeth's nature? He would discover something of it soon.

He leaped lightly against the wall, wedging his left foot into the crack between two foundation blocks. Before his impetus failed he kicked upwards and grabbed the window sill with his good hand. The off-center support disturbed his balance and his left side struck the wall with a dull thump. Pain tightened rather than loosened his grip, and he swung up through the window. He rolled head first into the room, favoring his wounded shoulder, and came to rest flat on his back on the plush carpet.

Liz Macnamara was awake. She sat curled on the sofa, as he had seen her before, and her face was white and frightened, again as before.

But her hands and feet were bound with tape and her mouth covered with a length of it. The terror in her eyes was immediate and deadly, for Floyd Rasmussen had one hand wound into her yellow hair and a squat black pistol pressed against the side of her head. His small, colorless eyes regarded Long. The wounded man lay still as a bronze statue.

"You shook my confidence earlier tonight, fella," remarked Rasmussen. "But at this distance I think I can't miss. Her, that is."

Long's eyes met Elizabeth's, and found within them an endless apology.

"Why? What is the purpose of this?" asked Long. His seemingly casual attempt to rise was checked by a movement of the gun. "I know about your financial enterprises, but between theft and murder there is a certain difference . . . They are crimes of different quality."

Rasmussen relaxed onto the couch, holding Liz's hair in a brutal fist. "True, but that bridge has been crossed," he stated. "Not by me, but that doesn't matter now."

The young woman's eyes closed in sick grief. Long's face was expressionless. "Mrs. Macnamara is dead?"

"My—partner—couldn't use her. He lost his temper." Rasmussen's words were resentful.

"Are you sure?" pressed Long. His frown was vaguely puzzled.

"Beat her up and throttled her," snapped Rasmussen. "I walked in just too late. Face all black and limp as a fish. Ugly." Liz Macnamara reeled and sagged in his grip. He ignored her.

"How unfortunate for all concerned," whispered Long.

"Yeah. I hadn't intended to kill anyone. I only wanted to keep Lizzie here incommunicado for a few weeks while I cleaned things up and got out. But life doesn't work right; Lizzie wrote a terrible letter and then she called her mother. And Doug, my partner: he's a vicious little asshole and he blew the simple job he was supposed to do. But all that's put me in a bind. So did you, leaving blood all over my house. Now I've got to get rid of both of you before I split."

"Where are you going?"

Rasmussen snorted. "Why should I tell you?"

"Because it doesn't matter," answered Long gently, looking away from Elizabeth's face. "If you're going to kill us it can't hurt you to tell."

He stared through the darkened dining area, where the Swedish glass shone like an assembly of ghosts. There was no sign of a struggle in the immaculate decor. The security chain on the front door hung unbroken. But then, Liz Macnamara had thought herself safe.

The white tape concealed half her face, but Long saw that Liz's jaw was clenched. Her blue eyes stared straight ahead of her. She appeared hard and angry. Remembering the words she'd spoken the previous evening, Long thought she was probably very much afraid.

The big man shrugged. "Okay. I got a yacht—the *Caroline*—remember the model in my office? And Threve's got a Cessna, hangared out in Marin. We'll be in Mexico this afternoon, and Sao Paulo tomorrow. Even with their inflation, two million dollars tax free makes it worthwhile learning another language."

"Why not simply leave us tied, then?" inquired Long, dispassionately. "You will be safe by the time we can free ourselves."

"Oh will I?" Rasmussen's voice was thick with sarcasm. "Fella I don't believe it. I saw what you did to the light switch in the bedroom, and how you tore apart the door. With the amount of blood you left in my plasterboard you ought to be dead—I've gutted enough deer to know how much a body holds."

"Then you must know I'm not about to dismember any more doors," sighed Long. Regardless of Rasmussen's gun, he sat up. "Not tonight."

"I don't know that at all," the blond man growled. He wound his fingers more tightly in Liz Macnamara's hair. "You're one weird cat. I don't know what it is: meditation, karate, hypnosis—but I have no idea what your limits are. I don't trust you. Also, you made me kill Blanco. I don't like you."

Mr. Long's smile expressed reciprocity. "But Miss Macnamara—you know she is no yogic adept. You needn't kill her."

Rasmussen laughed. Her head was twisted around by his beefy hand. "Liz? Liz has been living dangerously for months now. She's been having qualms of conscience. Besides, I know little Lizzie here. She carries a grudge. She'd follow me to hell, she would, simply to help the devil stoke the coals."

He sighed. "No. I'm not up for leaving behind either bodies or witnesses. Not after what Doug did."

Long's eyebrows rose. "How will you avoid that?"

"Simple. We're taking you along. On the *Caroline*. Part way.

"Get on your feet." He stood up, dragging the young woman with him. She thrashed against him, screaming muffled curses, but without her arms she could do nothing. Long regarded him without moving.

"Why should I cooperate with you?" he asked. "You offer me no incentive."

Rasmussen smiled and prodded the barrel of the gun against Liz's temple. "You'll do what I say because while you are alive there's a chance you might find an opportunity to get away. It's that simple. Of course I got no intention of giving you that opportunity, but you've got to bet the team you're on."

Long stood. The two men confronted one another in the yellow lamplight. "Do you think you could shoot the both of us before I could reach you?" he asked mildly.

"I don't have to," answered the heavy man, and his laughter rumbled through the rooms. "If you had the guts to sacrifice little Lizzie you would have gone for me long ago. That much we know about each other, Mr. Long. You know I'm able to kill her. I know you're not.

"That's why I'm the one in power."

Long's armour of composure broke momentarily at Rasmussen's last words, and a fire neither subtle nor civilized shone out of his narrow eyes. The burly blond flinched. He gestured with the gun.

"Walk. Out the back way, through the garage."

The fire vanished as though the furnace door had slammed shut. Long turned and preceded Rasmussen through the length of the house. They passed through a door in the kitchen.

The garage was so clean and empty as to appear unused. There were no cardboard boxes stacked against the wall, no broken venetian blinds. Not even a step-ladder.

Liz Macnamara had no old possessions: nothing of the sort one can't use and refuses to throw away. Until recently, she had been accustomed to owning nothing.

Within the garage the Mercedes sat in solitary splendor. Rasmussen tossed the keys to Long.

"Open the trunk," he commanded. Mr. Long did so. "Get her in."

Long stood motionless, keys in hand. "No."

Rasmussen's hand slid from Elizabeth's hair to her throat. It slowly tightened.

Liz opened her eyes wide as the pressure grew, but she did not look at Mayland Long. Her breath whistled in her nose and then that noise ceased.

"Stop," said Long. "There's no need for that."

Rasmussen was smiling broadly. He loosened his grip as Mr. Long bent to help to ease the bound woman into the trunk of the Mercedes. In a single, smooth motion he whipped the pistol around and struck Long on the back of the head.

The trunk door slammed shut on both his captives. "Goddamn," he said to himself. "Let's see what hypnosis can do about that!"

15

The solid thud of the trunk lock closed them both in darkness. Long groaned and eased his wounded side away from contact with the wall. His free hand sought and found Liz Macnamara's face. He pried the tape from her mouth, then began to free her hands.

"I'm sorry," she whispered. "I'm so very sorry."

"For what?" The bands of tape peeled away with difficulty; she swallowed a cry of pain.

"For what?" Long repeated. "It's I who have failed you, it seems, having entered the scene in the guise of a rescuer and succeeded only in adding to the defeat."

Her hands now free, Liz began to work on the bindings on her legs. "Floyd showed up about two hours ago. I let him in. I was sure he wouldn't risk . . . Oh hell!" Her voice began in outrage and faded.

"He told me you broke into his house, looking for me. I knew you were looking for Mother, of course. He said he shot you, and that you'd run off into the woods to die like an animal. He said his ceiling was soaked in blood."

The thunder of the engine starting delayed his reply. Acceleration pushed the prisoners against the back wall. The air was close and sour with metal and gasoline. "He hit me. That much is true, at any rate."

"Are you badly hurt?" Her hands blundered through the darkness. Found him.

"It's bandaged," said Mr. Long. One slim hand touched his injured shoulder. He enclosed it in his own hand and put it gently aside. "We have other things to worry about, now."

"I'm sorry," Elizabeth repeated helplessly. "If I

had not gotten involved with Rasmussen in the first place . . ."

"If any one of an infinite number of events had not happened in their sequence, the present would be a different place." He yawned. The trunk was getting warmer.

"Elizabeth, blame is a useless gesture. Regret is worse. Yet I regret that I am so weak and weary I may not be able to break the lock of the boot."

As he spoke his fingers tapped against metal, seeking the point of attachment.

"Break the lock? Of course you can't. It's steel."

"I can do a few parlor tricks," Long said drily. "Even against steel. But now . . ." He flattened his hand against the top of the rear wall of their prison.

"Ugh! I have nothing to brace against."

"Here." She put her back to the far wall and her hands pushed against the middle of his back.

"I think your bones would give before the steel lock," said Long, and at that moment the car turned right, rising onto two wheels, and the two of them were flung sideways and into one another's arms.

The intimacy was involuntary, and lasted only as long as the turn that caused it. When it was over the dark air was filled with silence. Then Long began to laugh.

It was a heavy, deep, spontaneous laughter, incongruous in a man so slight and lean, impossible from a man so injured. Mr. Long's laughter was like the cool thunder of a summer's afternoon and Liz Macnamara found herself smiling in the middle of her dread.

"Ah! Elizabeth. It's a very odd thing, to be a man."

His words challenged her and she found herself replying, "I've often thought so myself, but of course my knowledge is secondhand."

Without warning Long slammed the palm of his hand against the trunk lid. The lock snapped and a crack of light penetrated their prison. "Easier than I expected," he said.

Elizabeth wasted no time in compliments. She peered through the crack. "We're on 280," she stated. "Going north."

"Where is the *Caroline* docked?"

"North Beach. The marinas down here couldn't accommodate her." She settled back. "What are we going to do?"

Pushing with his feet against the trunk wall, Long edged closer. "We wait for an opportunity to jump."

"Out of a moving car?"

"When it stops, preferably." She saw a gleam of teeth in the darkness.

"You've never driven with Floyd Rasmussen," she retorted, feeling stung. Remembering the earlier interchange, she added, "What did you mean—when you said wasn't it funny to be a man?"

For a moment he did not respond, but rolled from his side to his back and lay staring at the metal ceiling. "I was referring to the species, not the sex.

"A man is an unusual being. He is capable of tremendous precision of thought. What is more, he creates—languages, philosophies, poetry . . . In short, he is the paragon of the animals. Yet he is so emminently—what is the right word?—distractable. During the most concentrated moments he may—no he *will*—float off like a butterfly and scatter all he has gained.

"Yet this is not a flaw in man, I think. This is what makes him man. And I must believe there is a value in that."

"Are you talking about me, or mankind in general?" she asked in a small, hurt voice.

He turned toward her. "I am talking about myself, Elizabeth." Seeing doubt in her face he continued, "You see, I have always been a collector—a hoarder of other people's ideas. I was not creative by nature. Not—distractable. It wasn't in me.

"But lately I have learned what it is to be human. Learned, but not understood. It seems to involve a great deal of misery crammed into a very short lifetime."

His voice was urgent, almost demanding, as he looked into Liz's eyes. "Why is that?" he asked.

"You're asking me?"

"Why not you, Elizabeth? You are human. Also, you may be the last person I will be able to ask."

She smiled and touched his face. "You should have asked my mother. I think she knew the answer to that."

"Ah, but I wasted my time in lesser matters. Though perhaps she told me after all." He shook his head. "I wish I could think more clearly."

"Your eyes," she whispered suddenly. "They glow in the dark."

"I wouldn't know about that."

She kissed him. "They do. How did Mother find you?"

Slowly he drew his head back. "We were introduced by a bartender at the James Herald Hotel—the fancy place you yourself paid for, Elizabeth. I live there."

"Is that how you find clients? Through the bartender?"

He stared a moment, uncomprehending. "Elizabeth. Do you also think I'm a professional detective?"

"You're not?" Liz Macnamara hit her head against the trunk lid. "Then what are you?"

Mayland Long sighed and smiled. "I am a friend. Of your mother's. I have no profession at all, merely sufficient money to live in comfort."

Being the person she was, Liz Macnamara cried, "To live in comfort! That's all I've ever wanted! How'd you get it?"

He hesitated. The tiny space echoed with road noise. "Out of a hole in the ground," he said finally.

"Oil?"

"No, Elizabeth. Gold."

"Oh! How free you must be."

She heard her own words. "I'm sorry. More sorry than I can say. The finest thing in my life was Mother, and because of me she's dead." Long shot a glance at her, frowning, but he held his tongue. "And you . . ."

"I am not dead yet," he replied, with a touch of acid. "And in no case do I wish to be added to your list of guilts."

"I have lived a long time, Elizabeth—longer than any creature on this earth can expect to live. These last years I have spent waiting for the fulfillment of a prophecy."

"A what?"

"A prophecy. And it has been fulfilled. I don't understand the sense of it, but then it was never said that I would understand—only that I would meet one who could show me the truth, and by that all I possessed I would lose."

Liz's eyebrows drew together. "What? Who was that, who could show you the truth, and take everything away . . ."

"Martha Macnamara showed me a rose." His words were quiet, almost drowned in the rumble of the engine. His face was turned slightly away.

She stared. "Are—were you in love with my mother?" Elizabeth whispered.

The word struck Long by surprise. "In love?" He considered it.

"Yes," he answered. "Your mother was the end of my waiting. But even had she not been a master of truth, had she only been the musician, the person she was . . ." He shook his head vainly. "But that's all one. Yes, I *am* in love with your mother, Elizabeth. Even now." His hands laced together over his face, concealing all but his black unreadable eyes.

"I . . ."

"And if you say you are sorry once more I may throw you out of the car." He turned his attention to the passing scenery.

* * *

"He's running the lights," observed Mr. Long.

"That's what I meant, about Floyd's driving. He never obeys the rules if he thinks he can get away with it.

"And he always speeds."

"We're now on Nineteenth Avenue, Elizabeth. Perhaps if I prop the boot open you can roll out at a corner."

"He'll see!"

"All the better. In order to prevent us, he would have to stop the car, and I am confident I could delay him while you run."

"My legs are both asleep. To the knees."

Long laughed again, as though all of time were before him, as though the day were bright. "We're a pretty pair," he said. "Three arms and two legs between us. Still, it can't be helped. Let's see how the fellow responds." He snapped the trunk open.

The answer was swift. The Mercedes shot forward as Rasmussen trod the accelerator and Long was nearly flung onto the pavement. He gripped the weather stripping and pulled himself back.

"Well, now we know," said Liz bleakly. "Would you rather break your neck or be drowned?"

"Such a limited choice!" cried Mayland Long. He sat upright, stretching his back with relief. The wind wake blew his black hair around his face. "Our hand is played, child. Sit here with me a while."

Liz Macnamara straightened painfully, propping the trunk open with one hand. She sat beside him. He put his arm around the young woman's shoulder, perhaps for support. Nineteenth Avenue shot away beneath them; streetlights, signs and automobiles fading into the past. The streetcar tracks beat against the wheels of the Mercedes. Rasmussen cut through the empty street at sixty miles per hour.

"There's a man—walking!" Liz waved her free hand and cried for help. The small figure vanished behind them. Rasmussen responded to her noise with a quick fishtale—left, then right across the lanes. The metal wall cracked her in the ribs.

"Goddamn him!" she shrieked, tears of anger in her eyes. Mr. Long's hand tightened reassuringly on her shoulder. His hand was warm.

"Why didn't you show up fifteen years ago," Elizabeth lashed out. "We needed you."

He drew back to look at her: perfect features, angelic hair, eyes like the sea. "You are a beautiful woman, Elizabeth. Like a painting, which is beauty of color, and like a sculpture, which is beauty of form. But you are alive, and have a beauty of movement which is more than these. Perhaps it is the beauty of music."

Before she could respond he added, "Do you remember Fred Frisch?"

"Fred? Of course I remember Fred. Class clown. We sat in the same classrooms for four years. Got the same grades, too, I think. How do you know Fred?"

He yawned and settled her against his good shoulder. "I met him a few days ago, while we were looking for you. This past night he . . . he kept me alive, I think."

"Fred?" she repeated helplessly. "Fred?"

"I like Fred Frisch," said Mr. Long.

This same Fred Frisch was sitting at his kitchen table, scrubbing blood-stained chair cushions. They really were ruined. He drizzled peroxide over the rusty blotches. It made a satisfactory hiss and bubble, but lifted the green dye from the ancient satin. By now the cushions were soaked through with his various attempts at cleaning. Probably they would mildew.

Fred sighed. He dropped the cushion, sighed again, dropped the pinkish rag and sighed once more. He did not know what to do.

He was gifted with a quick mind and a very simple emotional nature. He wanted to be loyal to Mr. Long. He was in awe of the man, who could endure such sickness and pain without breaking. Who managed to appear decisive in the middle of delirium. Who lay in this tatty living room so very close to dying—close as a military spec., was the way Fred put it—and spoke considerately, with impeccable manners. Who apologized to Fred for holding his arm too tightly.

And Jeez, that arm *still* ached.

He would have liked to *be* like Mr. Long, but he knew the stuff he himself was made of. He was just Fred, and the best he could do was to be loyal, and not blow the other man's game.

He stared at a cobweb high in the corner by the window and wondered whether being Chinese helped.

He carried the cushions back to the chair. Have to remember not to sit on them the next few days, till they dried. There, on the bright fabric where the seat cushion would rest, sat a small white cassette tape.

The story came back to him: the smashed recorder and the circle on the bathroom wall—which sign he would not have understood had not Long explained its Buddhist significance. This was the tape from the kidnapper's hole. He picked it up by one corner, as though it would bite. He took it to the kitchen.

He had four tape recorders in his small apartment. One took large tapes only and two did not work at all. The remaining unit had a bum recording head, but played back reasonably well. He dragged it from its place in the pile and plugged it in by the toaster. He rewound the tape and played it.

After a few minutes his shaking hand slammed down on the eject key. "Oh Jeezus."

The cries, the curses, punctuated by the thud of something hard against flesh . . . This was concentration camp stuff. This was murder.

The image of Mrs. Macnamara filled his mind—her old-fashioned braids, the bird-tilt of her head as she followed the toy car over the carpet. Her round, blue eyes, like Liz's eyes.

The face became Liz Macnamara's, delicate alabaster yet flushed with anger as she turned to counter some frat boy's silly cut. The memory was brief; it lasted as long as the action it recorded—Liz was most easily remembered in action.

Could she be dead? And her mother? Was this voice on the tape the voice of a dead woman—dying even as the tape ran? Fred's imagination quailed and the images faded into darkness.

He shuddered, and the table rattled in sympathy. He saw Mr. Long—the Black Dragon—as he had lain on the living room rug, unconscious. Here was another one who might be dead now. Or soon.

But the eyes in his memory opened. Brown eyes, heavy lidded, looked out calm and focused. They held Fred in place as though he were a rabbit.

No. The young man shook his thick pale hair. No sir, loyalty was one thing but life was another. Lives.

Fred hit rewind. He picked up the recorder with tape inside and snatched up his keys. As he locked the door behind him he rehearsed the story he had to give the police.

"The sea," whispered Mayland Long. "I smell it. And listen!"

"I don't hear anything but the car," Liz responded. "And I smell gas sloshing out of the tank. He's taking corners like a madman."

He drew her close to him, his single hand gripping her canvas belt. A screen of laurel appeared at the left, very close to the car. The leaves rustled in the breeze—a sea breeze, foretelling the dawn. "It is time for you to leave us," Long announced. "Please double tie your belt, so that it doesn't come loose."

Mystified, Liz complied with his order. "What do you mean—time for me to leave? We're going too fast, still. And what about you? I'll bet you could survive jumping a lot better than I could."

The pressure against her waist increased. She was lifted from the sheet metal. "Ouch! Please! You're twisting me all around. What are you doing?"

"I'm sorry," said Mr. Long, in unconscious parody of Elizabeth herself. "But it is difficult with only one arm."

"What is?" she began, as the Mercedes, following the angle of the road, went into a hard right turn. In answer, Long braced his feet against the right wall of the trunk and flung his companion out of the car and into the shrubby trees.

Her shriek of surprise faded—like all else—into the past.

16

The drive leading to North Beach Marina cut through an immaculate lawn. The Mercedes careened into it, skidding on gravel. The sky above the ocean was clear and black; the moon was setting, tinged mustard yellow. To the east, however, where the far shore of the Bay lay hidden, the darkness was dull and linty, and the stars were fading. As the Mercedes' nose dipped down toward the piers, its lights flashed three times.

Rasmussen maintained his breakneck speed along the straight entryway, then jammed the brakes. Before the car had stopped moving he was out the door and running. He dropped to one knee behind the open trunk, bracing his pistol with his forearm.

A smaller shape sprinted up the road to join him. In the distance, dogs began to bark.

"All right, folks. Get out here, now!" snarled the big blond. Threve, standing beside Rasmussen, hissed, "What the hell happened, Floyd? You got Liz in there?"

"No. Just me," answered Long, climbing wearily to his feet. He ignored Rasmussen to consider Threve.

Threve glared in turn at Long over the gleaming barrel of an automatic.

The prisoner spoke. "We haven't been introduced. My name is Mayland Long. I know that your name is Threve. And I'm told that you are a murderous thug." His words were easy, urbane, almost cordial. "I've come to make sure it is true."

Threve inched closer to Rasmussen. "This is—is this the weird guy?"

Rasmussen nodded. "Where's Liz?" he snapped.

"Far away," Long answered placidly. He lifted his head to the breeze. The moonlight shone on his glossy black hair.

Rasmussen's teeth ground together. "Then she's dead," he stated. "I didn't slow down under fifty the entire trip."

"Why the hell didn't you lock the goddamn trunk?" roared Threve, stung by the prisoner's attitude and furious at Rasmussen as well. The chorus of barking rose with his voice.

Rasmussen divided his attention; he trusted neither man.

"I don't think she was injured," said Long. "She landed in a bush."

"Shit! You said you had her, Floyd! How the hell did you let her get away?"

Floyd Rasmussen did not answer. He locked eyes with Long, who smiled grimly. "Why her and not you?" Rasmussen asked.

Mr. Long turned his face to the water. "I came to see Mrs. Macnamara. Til I find her, my business with you isn't done."

"It is, because you are," growled Rasmussen, shifting his grip on the black pistol. His eyes were doubtful. "Hell of a price to pay."

Long smiled. "You don't even know what I'm buying."

The dogs were silent suddenly; perhaps their master had come out to hush them. Only a chorus of crickets sounded at the edge of hearing, like the blood pounding in Rasmussen's ears. The pistol didn't waver, but he stared warily at Long, afraid that his prisoner had plans that he, Rasmussen, did not understand.

Threve answered for Rasmussen. "Wings and a halo, that's all. Plug him, Floyd, and let's get out of here. If that bitch gets to the police . . ."

Rasmussen hesitated, gazing into pale brown eyes under the light of a gold moon.

Douglas Threve was a less complicated man and so less vulnerable to doubt. He cursed and raised his own weapon slightly. Without warning Long struck him in the chest and knocked the small man over the gravel path. Threve's pretty automatic went sailing into the brush of the hill. Long rolled onto his back and grabbed Threve by the throat.

The small man's shout of surprise and rage was cut off cleanly. His hands clawed vainly at Long's face. Threve's heels kicked against the gravel.

As soon as Long moved, Rasmussen was free of his paralysis. He leaped for the struggling pair and swung the butt of the pistol at Long's head. The first blow caught his victim on the right shoulder.

Long dropped Threve, and he turned upon Rasmussen a glare of enduring, patient hate. The blond raised his pistol again, and Long's hand rose toward this other enemy in what seemed to be as much a gesture of malediction as an attempt at defense. His fingers were spread wide, and in the moonlight his hand looked like the talon of some gigantic raptor. Rasmussen remembered the odd grip of Long's hand on his own and he shuddered, not knowing what it was that he fought. But the pistol in his hand was falling, and it caught Long above the temple.

"See?" hissed the blond at his partner, who lay dazed at the edge of the path, gulping air. "Who's a fool? I told you about this guy."

"Shoot him now," gagged Threve. "Shoot him or I will."

"With what?" Rasmussen stuffed his pistol in a jacket

pocket. "We don't need more noise." He straddled Long and tore open the front of his shirt. The hunter examined Long's bandages. "So that's where I got him. He was crawling toward me in the dark, like a big lizard. I wonder if he did this himself. I don't see how."

Rasmussen brooded. "I don't like that. He can't have gone to the police, or they'd never have let him go in a condition like this. But it means he had help, somewhere."

From his other pocket Rasmussen pulled a short skinning knife and a roll of adhesive tape. He cut away Fred Frisch's handiwork and bound Long's two hands together, winding tape from the wrist halfway up to the elbow.

"Shoot him already," insisted Threve, trying to stand.

"No shooting. I could cut his throat here and now, if I wanted. In fact he may be dead already. Ought to be.

"But I tell you Doug, this guy's like a snake. No matter what you do to it, it'll wriggle till nightfall."

Threve sneered. "It's already nightfall. It's almost dawn," he answered sourly. "What are we gonna do about it?"

Rasmussen smacked his hands on his thighs and stood.

"We're going to do what we planned. Dump them both off the Farallons, tied to concrete blocks. Live or dead, this guy can play with the lobsters."

"Help me carry him," grunted Rasmussen, bending to lift. "No. Never mind," he reconsidered, feeling the lightness of the burden. "You get ready to sail." He started toward the water, plodding awkwardly, the limp form of his prisoner over one shoulder. Clouds of dust rose like smoke with every shuffling footstep.

"I lose my gun and you start giving orders, huh?" rasped Threve. He touched his bruised neck gingerly.

Rasmussen sighed. "You want to tote him?"

Threve spat onto the dry road. "I had to carry the mother."

"You wouldn't have, if you hadn't beat her to death. Or strangled her." His steps echoed on wood.

Threve swallowed his rage, stalking ahead along the pier.

The *Caroline* was a beautiful ship, even with all sails tightly furled. She was five tons of teak, trimmed in brass, and though she was primarily a sailing ship, she had the power to drive fifteen knots in calm seas.

The night was failing when Long opened his eyes. The first cries of gulls broke through the deep cough of the engine. His head hurt and his vision was blurry.

He regarded his arms, wound in a tube of white tape. Any attempt to pull them apart sent intolerable pain shooting up his left arm and shoulder. He tried to pull his feet under him and found they were also bound— tied with wire to a large concrete block.

Next to him lay a bundle in a green oilcloth tarp. It was also tied to the block. After a moment's confusion he knew what that bundle had to be. He sat up and looked closer at it, forced finally to believe. Thoughts resounded through the hollows of his skull. He listened to them without interest.

So he was like other men in this way too. He believed what he wanted to believe: what he felt he had to believe. Until, of course, time slammed him into the meaningless truth. Martha was dead and he was going to die. Even without these men and their absurd, murderous thievery, he would die soon, for he was old and his search was over.

He'd found what he sought. Truth. He had no questions any more. It was not what he wanted, said a small voice within him, but it was what he'd chased so long.

The little man by the cave in Honan must have been mad, to appear so happy. Knowledge of the truth led only to despair.

He extended his hands and raucous, lancing pain mixed into the cries of the gulls. He pulled the oilcloth gently away from Martha Macnamara's face.

That face was lacerated and bruised purple, and about

the nose and mouth were marks like sunburn. Her long hair, grizzled brown and white, lay tangled over her forehead. He brushed the hair away.

"Ah, Martha," he whispered. "I can't believe three days was enough."

He stroked the sad, mottled face. "I had a question to ask. I'd saved it for centuries. When I met you I wasted my time with play, and I did not ask it. No matter." He swallowed painfully. "The play was more important."

The *Caroline* dipped into a wave as it left the shelter of the Bay and cut into the Pacific. Long raised himself up and peered west, into the wind.

So this was the rapprochement with the sea he had avoided for so long. Waves slapped the wood, sullenly. Long still did not understand water.

He'd traded his future for the chance to say good-bye to a woman who was already dead. That farewell had been important. But why?

Was anything important, here on the edge of the irremedial loss? Cold air filled his lungs. His breath steamed. He heard the two men moving about in the bow of the boat, but he did not take his eyes from the sea.

The horizon to the right and behind him was streaked with brilliance. The near side of each wave glistened. He sat in a quiet which was divorced from both pain and joy. Even his curiosity had left him.

Gaunt black rocks broke through the waves in the distance ahead. A few ships dotted the water far from shore.

He took one of Martha's cold hands in his own and looked again at her face.

Suddenly he started, held his breath, and leaned toward her. Again he saw the small cloud of white fog dissolve against the green tarpaulin. He lifted her head on his hand and whispered, "Martha?"

Blue eyes opened, brighter than the dawn sky. They wandered unfocused. "Who?"

"M–Mayland Long," he whispered, stumbling over his own name.

Her hands floundered in the tarp, like those of a baby in swaddling. "Oh!" Like a baby, her eyes were blue and vague. "I've . . . I've been so worried. About you."

He stripped away the oilcloth, shaking her gently to keep her awake. "There is something I must ask you," he began.

With great effort, she raised her head. "About Liz? My daughter. Did you call the police?"

She lifted herself further, grimacing. "What's wrong with your hands?" Martha blinked and began to look around her.

"Your daughter is safe, I trust." He spoke eagerly, his voice unsteady. "I left her in a bush. I haven't called the police, although Fred may have. Must have, by now.

"But hear me, Martha. What I want to say, is that I love you. Is that all right with you?"

Martha Macnamara took in all this without blinking. Her smile was a painful, cracked thing. "Of course, Mayland. I'm delighted to hear it, because I love you." She tried to laugh and collapsed to the deck in dizziness. "Couldn't you tell?"

He closed his eyes and gave a sigh that was half a growl. In one fluid motion he got to his feet. The wire around his ankles restrained him, and he suddenly remembered their perilous situation. Carelessly, he reached down and snapped the wire.

Mayland Long smiled, and the red sun broke over the hills to the southeast. His lips drew back from his teeth and he held his bound arms out before him. White tape caught the new light and his bronze skin glowed. He threw back his head and laughed—a laugh neither English nor Chinese, but filled with glad thunder. The tape gleamed ruddy in the sunlight, and as he strained against it it fell away like charred paper.

His injured arm fell to his side. The right hand he extended, impossible fingers spread wide, as though he would grab the sun. All pain and weakness were gone, drowned in a flood of simple joy.

He heard running footsteps and turned.

"He sure ain't dead!" shouted Douglas Threve, who stood before Long holding a heavy steel wrench. "I'll fix that!"

Long dodged the blow smoothly and struck Threve's arm. The wrench clattered on the deck.

Long struck again. His fingers closed around Threve's neck, thumb pressed under the chin. He lifted Threve quickly, and with the motion one makes to flick open a cigarette lighter, Long snapped the man's neck. He tossed the body aside.

Floyd Rasmussen stood before him, braced against the cabin wall. The barrel of the pistol that he held was shaking.

Long caught his eye. "You know better than that." He spoke gently, chiding. He heard behind him Martha crawl out of her rutch of oilcloth.

Rasmussen licked his lips and slid down against the wall. "God! Can't you be killed?"

"Oh yes," answered Long. "But not disposed of. If you kill me you will have me with you forever."

"Hypnosis," stated Rasmussen without conviction.

"No one has been killed, here, except this man. Who is my responsibility." Long's voice was measured and reasonable. It held the blond man pinned against the wall. "Now you have the opportunity you thought was lost forever. No past murder forces you to shoot. If you do, it will be a fresh decision, and will seal your future once again."

Waves slapped against the pilotless craft, turning it out of its course. Wind whistled in the rigging.

"No one is dead? The mother . . ." Rasmussen looked wildly about. Long stepped aside to reveal the empty wrappings. "She is risen. She is not here," he whispered.

Rasmussen dropped the gun and put both hands to his head. Instantly Long dived for the cabin wall and brought Rasmussen down. The big man clawed ineffectually against the single lean brown hand which closed upon his throat. He gasped and choked. Long's face was set and deliberate. He reached his thumb under Rasmussen's jaw.

"Oolong. No." Martha Macnamara spoke with authority. "All you said to him is true. I don't want you to carry him as a burden for the rest of your life."

He raised his face to hers. His eyes flared yellow: feral, merciless. Her own eyes were half closed in a puffy face.

"It'll be nothing new to me."

"No!" she repeated, unwavering. Blue eyes and gold eyes met: two colors of flame. "Everything is new, forever," she stated. "It is always the first time."

The gold eyes dropped and the black head bowed. Martha's hands went gingerly to her head. She winced, groaning.

Mayland Long cleared his throat. "Then, Martha, I suggest you search Mr. Rasmussen's pockets for the adhesive tape he carries . . .

"And there will be a small hunting knife by it. Be careful."

She bound Rasmussen while Long held him down by the neck, feeling panic pulse beneath his hand. When Martha was done they both stood and walked to the stern.

"Can you handle a boat?" inquired Martha.

"Not at all," was the prompt answer.

Her broken lips tried to smile. "I can't believe there is something you can't do." Her hands sought out a tangled, fallen braid and began to work it free.

"I have avoided travel by water," answered Long, as a swell pitched the *Caroline* sideways.

"Because of another prophecy?"

"Because I get sick," he replied. Only a narrow band of dark iris was visible as a smile spread from his eyes to his mouth. "And because I'm afraid of water. Can you,

Martha? Handle a boat? The question is of more than academic interest."

She shrugged. Her blue dress was creased and stained. It had lost half its buttons. "I can turn the wheel."

Liz Macnamara sat at the sergeant's desk as the officers of the day patrol came on duty. She was acutely aware of her dishabille. The sergeant himself sat in another room, behind a glass door, talking on the phone. He had been in there for the last ten minutes.

She heard that door open. "Miss Macnamara," he began. "That's M—a—c—n—a—m—a—r—a?"

"Yes, yes! You have all that."

"Don't get excited, Miss." He picked up a pencil and bounced the eraser end a few times against the desk blotter.

"What do you mean?" Liz wailed. "They've killed my mother! They're going to kill . . ."

"Mr. Long. Mayland Long, M—a—y—l—a—n—d," interjected the sergeant. His eyes were sleepy, his girth considerable.

"Yes, that's his name."

"And your mother's first name is Martha?"

"Oh God, yes, what of it? *Do* something."

"We have," the policeman said. "Two days ago a Mr. Mayland Long reported your mother missing. He didn't have anything more for us to go on, so there wasn't much we could do, but an hour ago a kid walked in on the Palo Alto police with a crazy story about this man Long. And a tape. Since then all the departments on the Peninsula have been on the alert.

" 'Course, we hadn't thought to check the Bay until you came to us with your information, Miss Macnamara."

"Thrown into a tree?" He dropped the pencil.

The young woman before him wriggled in her seat. There was a leaf sticking out of her hair, a long slender leaf like a donkey's ear. Her arms were scratched and that bathrobe deserved an R rating.

The sergeant was a fan of old movies. He couldn't decide whether Liz Macnamara looked more like Marlene Dietrich or Greta Garbo, but despite her tangled hair and grease smears she sure looked like something.

"Tree or bush. A laurel. In Golden Gate Park. What does it matter?" Liz folded her arms tightly, hugging herself.

"I'm sorry about your mother," the sergeant said.

Liz nodded miserably.

"And considering what you've said about your relationship with these two kidnappers I think you need a lawyer."

"Hell with that," moaned the young woman. The sergeant's mouth twitched sympathetically.

"Still, there's not much more I can say to you until you're represented by counsel . . ."

At that moment the outer door opened and Fred Frisch walked in, carrying his tape recorder and tugging on his moustache. Seeing Liz, he escaped the guiding hand of the officer who had brought him in, and he picked his way among the desks to her.

"I'm sorry, Liz," he began. "I tried . . . I mean, do you remember me at all?"

She stood, examining him closely. Loose jointed, with limp blond hair, and eyes like a Bassett Hound: was this the fellow who had saved Long's life? "Of course, Fred. Mr. Long talked about you tonight. He said you . . . kept him going."

"You've seen him since? Is he . . ."

She shook her head. "I'm afraid they've killed him by now. They killed my mother." She sagged back into the chair. "And it's all my fault."

Fred swallowed. "Hey. It's not that way. I know all about it. I found your disk file at RasTech and printed it."

She glanced up in amazement and Fred shifted from foot to foot. "He wanted me to. Mr. Long—the Black Dragon."

"The what?"

Ignoring the sergeant behind his desk, Fred dragged a

chair across the floor and sat. "His name is really Black Dragon, in Chinese. I really admire the guy, you know?"

"He liked you," responded Elizabeth, blinking away tears.

"Did he say that?"

"Yes, and that he loved my mother. But they're going to kill him. Even he thought so, when he threw me out of the car."

"I don't know," said Fred, frowning and blowing out his moustache. "He's a hard man to kill."

Liz turned to him with the dawning of real curiosity. "Have you always had that moustache?" she asked.

"Hummm," snorted the sergeant behind his desk.

Martha held the glossy, many-spoked wheel, leaning against it. The fat red sun had climbed a few degrees into the sky, and she had turned the nose of the *Caroline* toward it. Daylight touched the cold water, making the air milky with fog.

Mayland Long stood beside her with a glass of water in his hand. She started, for she had not heard him approach. Gratefully, she took the glass and drank from it.

"Oh yes, that's better," she said. He stood behind her and said nothing.

"Talk to me, Mayland. My head hurts."

His answer came slowly. "I can't think of anything to say." With great care he ran his finger through her loose hair, combing it. Martha's battered features eased into a smile. "I can't braid it for you without my other hand."

"That feels wonderful," she murmured, peering into the pale obscurity at small dark shapes that had not been there a minute ago. Were they rocks?

She shivered. "I think I've been cold forever."

"There I can help," chuckled Mayland Long, and he put his arm around her waist as he pressed her body against his.

"Oh my!" she exclaimed. "You're a furnace!" She touched his bare arm wonderingly. It was smooth, with no trace of the sticky tape. It radiated heat. He bent his face over hers. It, too, was very warm.

"So hot! You've used yourself up," she said.

He raised his head and stared out. "No, I'm not quite used up. But I thought I was, early this morning." Frowning, he added, "My understanding was . . . imperfect." A movement on the water distracted him.

"Look." She did so. One of the dark shapes in the fog had become a boat, a Coast Guard cutter. It veered by the bow of the *Caroline*, which bobbed in the faster boat's wake.

Mr. Long strode to the stern to turn off the engine, that being the only action in their power to assist the boarders, while Mrs. Macnamara smoothed her dress. With old-fashioned courtesy and a certain degree of self-satisfaction, they welcomed their rescuers aboard.

17

The door opened to Martha's triplet knock. In Long's sitting room rain beat against the windows, but a tall lamp was lit, and soft light drew a circle around the antique gold chairs.

"I just called the hospital and they said you checked out. You weren't supposed to do that; the doctors said you weren't ready."

Mayland Long smiled quietly, almost shyly, at Martha and ushered her in. Except for the cotton sling around his right arm, he looked as he had a week ago: a slight Eurasian man of indeterminate age, whose dark features faded into the shadows of the room.

"They didn't like their test results," he stated. "I didn't like their tests. We were, neither of us, happy about the other, so I came home. Have you seen Elizabeth today? Have they set bail?"

Martha sank into the nearest of the chairs. "She's out on her own recognizance, because she turned herself in. I visited her this morning, before the rain started. That young man was there—the one with the talking car—I mean the car you talk to.

"I hope Liz won't have to go to prison." Martha's small jaw was set and her forehead creased with worry. "But I think the judge will be lenient, under the circumstances." Her face in the lamplight showed every trace of the mistreatment she had suffered. She smiled a round-faced smile as he pulled his chair beside her and took her hand in his.

"How long have you been . . . a human being?" she asked him.

He glanced from her face to the gray world outside. "Less than a week, I think."

She snorted. "You know what I mean."

He looked back to her. "Six years ago I found an old man in the hills outside Taipei. He was a master of Tao: not my master, he informed me, but nonetheless he was very wise."

Martha Macnamara frowned. "Tell me. I don't approve of mysteries."

Long looked down at his hands. His lean face expressed doubt. "What do you know of dragons, Martha."

" 'How many times,' " she quoted, " 'have I entered the cave of the green dragon!' "

He turned halfway, and looked away from the brooding weather. "Delusion. Yes. But I don't speak of a green dragon, but a black one."

"An imperial dragon?" she questioned in turn.

He turned full toward her. "So you know about the dragon of five fingers?"

She laughed at the eagerness in his words. "Oh, I've been around the block once or twice. The black dragon is a scholar. He was claimed as the ancestor of every ruling family of China. The black dragon lives forever."

He met her eyes as he added, "But I will not."

Martha's chin rose and she spoke with conviction. "Living forever," she began, "is what makes *all* dragons delusion, whether they're green, red or black. Life is a moment long, no more. If you hold on to it, you're lost!"

Gently he withdrew his hand and lay it on his lap. He leaned back in the chair and closed his eyes to the light.

"I hold on to everything," he remarked. "I always have."

"Back when you knew Bodhidharma?"

"Yes, Martha." His eyes opened and one neat brow went up. "Did you think I lied to you?"

"And the son of Thomas Rhymer? The fairy host?" she pressed him.

"I did not claim to be an eyewitness to those events. I just repeated the story as told." He smiled broadly.

"Meeting the man who sat in front of a wall—the one you call Bodhidharma—changed a life which till then had been devoted to the traditional pursuits of dragons . . ."

"Which are?"

"Mmph! Scholarship, calligraphy, collecting objects d'art . . ."

"That's all? Sounds pretty thin."

"Also devouring oxen, tigers, and occasionally people." His smile remained intact.

"Better . . . I wouldn't mind living like that," said Martha.

"Yes, it is agreeable, on the surface. But I developed a fascination for man—tiny, helpless, short-lived creature that he was—because he created the beautiful things I could only copy. And hoard. Dragons, you see, are not very creative. We have never been great painters or poets, but instead great collectors.

"I wished to know what it was that gave man the power to do what he does—to paint, to write poetry, to sit for nine years facing a wall. . . ." His words trailed off.

"Bodhidharma told me, Martha, that he was seeking

truth. I thought about that for quite some time. I went from teacher to teacher. At first my quest was to find out what there was in man to make him act so strangely: to desire an abstract nothing with a passion that should be reserved for gold. But eventually I came to see that I would only find out the truth *about* man by finding man's truth itself!"

Long's right hand played with the whistle of the teapot. His teeth shone and his opaque eyes were dancing. "Dogbreeders grow to look like dogs," he said. "And slowly, over centuries, I became like the creature I studied, growing apart from my own kind.

"If I met a dragon now, I'd have nothing to say to him!"

"Cats don't like cats," interjected Martha.

Mayland Long shot one mischievous glance at her and was obliged to look away. He was grinning hugely.

"I have spent decades in frozen caves in what is now Nepal," he announced. "I have coiled by stone beehive cells in Leicester. I have corresponded with the Dean of St. Paul's. Not the present dean, of course . . ."

"Of course not. You mean Donne."

He grunted assent. "The men I sought were those who seemed to have found what Bodhidharma found beneath the cave wall. That indescribable formless whatever . . . truth!

"Around me my kind faded. I hardly noticed. Dragons are not social by nature. (I am the exception.) My interest—my obsession—kept me alive.

"But I did not find truth," he concluded, without irony.

Martha Macnamara lay her hands against his face. "Don't you know that you yourself *are* the truth walking?"

He kissed the palm of one hand, then the other. "A dragon cannot make sense of such a statement," he said. "But now . . ."

The moment's silence was filled with the sleepy drone of the rain. The circle of light was small.

"I know," he began slowly, "that you are my master."

She laughed. "If you insist. But I would rather be your mistress."

"That too."

Thunder rolled in the distance. Mayland Long turned to the window. He walked over and pressed his hand against the glass. "It rarely thunders in California. The night I lost—that I became a human being—it crashed incessantly.

"I had heard about a Taoist teacher who was very wise. His name was Yung Chung-jo; he was a retired military man. When I found him he was sitting on a bare hilltop, wearing his tattered old dress uniform. He had come there in order to die.

"He was not afraid. I coiled about him and shielded him from the rain.

"I told him about my search, where it had begun and where it had led me. I told him what scriptures I had read, and in which transcriptions, for I had learned all the major human languages to aid me in my task. I listed the names of all the teachers I had had previously and repeated the advice they had given me. I wanted to be clear and exact with Yung, because I had failed with so many before.

"And the old man laughed at me—he laughed as I think only the Chinese can laugh, when they mock a person. It's terrible, the way they can laugh. It can reduce one to . . ." He glanced toward Martha and continued gently. "You are laughing at me now, Martha. That's all right. I know what sort of fool I am.

"Then he told me he was not destined to be my master, because he was dying. He said my master would be one who had more *chi*—more strength—than I. And he foretold that when I met my master, all I had gathered would be taken from me.

"He sat in the rain through the night, while I slept coiled about him. In the morning, when I awoke, I looked like this, and in my arms I was holding a dead man."

"It must have hurt, to become human," she whispered, holding out her hand to him.

Mr. Long came back into the light. "It still hurts," he said.

Lightning snapped in the sky and again thunder rumbled. "What shall I do, Martha? Where shall I live? How shall I spend my time?"

Martha Macnamara took a deep breath and sat straight in the chair. She was wearing her respectable tweeds. "I am not the Queen of Elfland," she began.

"You are more beautiful, Martha. And you possess more *chi.*"

She ignored the interruption. "But if you come with me I will treat you better than she did the Rhymer."

He pulled her to her feet and kissed her, slowly and with great concentration. Their hands were bathed in yellow light. Their faces, above the lamp, were shadowed. "Still," he whispered in her ear, "he came back with truth on his tongue."

She giggled. "It doesn't belong there."

"Then what will my mistress teach me?" He kissed her cheek, the corner of her eye, her forehead . . .

Martha Macnamara took a step back and looked up at Mayland Long. "Why, to play the piano, of course!" She held up his dark slender hand. "How wonderful!"

FANTASY AND SCIENCE FICTION FAVORITES

Bantam brings you the recognized classics as well as the current favorites in fantasy and science fiction. Here you will find the most recent titles by the most respected authors in the genre.

☐	25260	THE BOOK OF KELLS R. A. MacAvoy	$3.50
☐	25122	THE CHRISTENING QUEST	$2.95
		Elizabeth Scarborough	
☐	24370	RAPHAEL R. A. MacAvoy	$2.75
☐	24169	WINTERMIND Parke Godwin, Marvin Kaye	$2.75
☐	23944	THE DEEP John Crowley	$2.95
☐	23853	THE SHATTERED STARS Richard McEnroe	$2.95
☐	23575	DAMIANO R. A. MacAvoy	$2.75
☐	25403	TEA WITH THE BLACK DRAGON R. A. MacAvoy	$2.95
☐	23365	THE SHUTTLE PEOPLE George Bishop	$2.95
☐	24441	THE HAREM OF AMAN AKBAR	$2.95
		Elizabeth Scarborough	
☐	20780	STARWORLD Harry Harrison	$2.50
☐	22939	THE UNICORN CREED Elizabeth Scarborough	$3.50
☐	23120	THE MACHINERIES OF JOY Ray Bradbury	$2.75
☐	22666	THE GREY MANE OF MORNING Joy Chant	$3.50
☐	25097	LORD VALENTINE'S CASTLE Robert Silverberg	$3.95
☐	20870	JEM Frederik Pohl	$2.95
☐	23460	DRAGONSONG Anne McCaffrey	$2.95
☐	24862	THE ADVENTURES OF TERRA TARKINGTON	$2.95
		Sharon Webb	
☐	23666	EARTHCHILD Sharon Webb	$2.50
☐	24102	DAMIANO'S LUTE R. A. MacAvoy	$2.75
☐	24417	THE GATES OF HEAVEN Paul Preuss	$2.50

Prices and availability subject to change without notice.

Buy them at your local bookstore or use this handy coupon for ordering: